BLACK BONES JONES

Ex-slave. Ex-soldier. Exorcist.

JAMES MOORER

DARK ANTHEM PRESS

Copyright © 2024 by James Moorer
All rights reserved.

This book is entirely a work of fiction. Any references to historical events, real people, or real places are used fictitiously. Other names, characters, places, and events are products of the author's imagination. Any resemblance to actual events, places, or persons, living or dead, is entirely coincidental. No artificial intelligence (A.I.) or predictive language software was used in any part of the creation of this book.

No portion of this book may be reproduced in any form without written permission from the publisher or author, except as permitted by U.S. copyright law. It is illegal to copy this book, post it to a website, or distribute it by any other means without permission. The author expressly prohibits using this work in any manner for purposes of training artificial intelligence technologies to generate text, including without limitation, technologies that are capable of generating works in the same style or genre as this work. The author reserves all rights to license uses of this work for generative AI training and development of machine learning language models.

Created and printed in the United States of America.

First edition 2024
Published by Dark Anthem Press, an imprint of One Moorer LLC.
Author photo by Kris Garfield
Cover design by Drew Foerster & Laura Davis

Identifiers: 979-8-9911025-4-4 (hardcover) | 979-8-9911025-2-0 (ebook) | 979-8-9911025-1-3 (paperback) | 979-8-9911025-3-7 (audiobook)
Subjects: *Horror*—Fiction | *Western*—Fiction | *Supernatural*—Fiction | *Paranormal*—Fiction | *U.S. History*—1845-1865—Fiction

PROLOGUE

There comes with all things of men, that which is known and that which is truth. Neither is exclusive nor bound to the other, especially when stirred by man's ambition—that siren's call in the pit of one's soul. But it ain't never the voice of God that whispers to a man to make his fortune on the backs of others. That voice comes from a darker place.

It was that dark, insatiable hunger for power which led many men to seek their manifest destiny, like a parasite twisting their souls, and drew them to the distant shores of *Alkebulan*, known as Africa. They took millions of people, hailing from nations whose names have been lost in the sands of time, and enslaved them in the New World. Their unquenchable greed blinded them to the callous brutality of owning another human, and unleashed an unspeakable darkness upon the land, themselves, and their lineage. Their benightedness set free supernatural forces upon an unsuspecting continent; an ancient power not meant to be wielded by unsanctified hands. And those who called themselves master would know the darkest meaning of the word slave.

But God is not so unkind as to leave man to his own damnation. Despite being enslaved, there were some among the descendants of Alkebulan who had been born not to fear the terror by night nor the pestilence that walked in darkness. They carried with them The Knowing, an inner wisdom which held the power to stand against all unholy manner of perdition that sought to claim the souls of man. For generations, shamanic elders secretly transferred The Knowing to their successors under the cover of the moon. And to the children of Alkebulan, these spiritual heirs of The Knowing were called *Adjani*.

ONE

— • —

JONES PLANTATION, ALABAMA 1845

I t was hot and humid, as all sweltering summer nights were in
Birmingham, Alabama. The air felt thick and stifling, and even
the gentlest of breezes was a sweet release. For much of the South
in 1845, this was the state of most nights. But this night would
be like no other. This night would be both a blessing and curse,
especially for the residents of the Jones Plantation. A sprawling,
pristine, forty-acre canvas on the portrait of early America, green
and glowing.

On this moonless solstice, in the mythic haze of night, a spectacle
like no other was unfolding. Tiny lights rose into the night sky
above the plantation's main house, dancing like fireflies on whatever wind gave them purchase. But these angelic sparkles of light
were not the magic of God's hand. They were the remnants of a
burning flame.

The home of Malachi Jones, passed down from father to son and
from father to son before him, would see its last day on earth. Once
a jewel of Southern life and luxury and the pride of Jessup County,
the Jones Plantation was now a bonfire. It burned like a righteous
fire, a blaze whose light could be seen from the fields in three coun-

ties. Not a single structure was spared by the raging behemoth, as it moved from building to building like an incandescent serpent devouring anything and everyone in its path.

As Malachi fell to his knees with a pitchfork plunged in his back, he bore witness to a grisly visage of destruction that spared not even his wife and children. With his last dying breath, he sputtered a faint prayer to the Almighty. For Malachi knew this was the bitter crop he had sown, and the last sight his eyes would see was that of the slave quarters.

Black men and women ran in all directions, trying to escape the inferno. The roar of the howling fire drowned out their pitiful screams. Some fell, engulfed in flames, while others less fortunate remained trapped inside shack houses that were consumed from floor to ceiling. But it wasn't the fire that made some drop dead in fear, it was something far more terrifying. It was a creature, something beyond human, that seemed to have spawned from hell itself.

This fresh hell rose as an inky Black Figure, its arms long and other-worldly, with a dark, faceless form in a gown of black as pitch. Its very touch ignited anything or anyone within reach. Children wailed as friends and family fell in scorching, ashen heaps. The Dark Figure pitied no one, respecting neither slave nor master like some avenging angel sent to deliver judgment on them all.

Amidst the chaos, a woman, Esther. A slave of thirty years. Stalwart and uncannily steadfast, she emerged with eyes that belied the fear coursing through every fiber of her being. While all that she knew burned around her, she placed herself between those she loved, and the Figure, hellbent to destroy them all. But Esther had a purpose of her own.

With her hands clutching a necklace of bones around her neck, Esther shouted.

"You'll not have me and mine this night, demon!"

The Inky Figure hissed as it turned its spiny fingers toward Esther.

"From whence ye came must ye return!" Esther shouted.

A crowd gathered behind them; the remnants of overseers and slaves, too afraid to flee, watched as Esther stood like a David before this unholy Goliath. They murmured and wailed about what might befall them should she fail. For none among them was brave enough to stand with her, lend a shoulder of support or a word of encouragement. All that is, save her son.

Jacob Jones, Esther's ten-year-old son, was fortunate enough to have been sired by the man she called husband. Eyes like his mother, his steely gaze was transfixed on the only woman he loved more than life itself. And with his father's death long past, Jacob bore the weight of manhood at a time when his tender and strange life should have known few cares. But he was a slave child, and a slave's life was like a strand of wheat in a tempest, a whirlwind that knew no end.

Esther chanted aloud in Amharic, her native African tongue.

"Menifesini āsiralehu!!!" She shook the bone necklace before her. "Menifesini āsiralehu!!!"

Suddenly, the Inky Figure faltered, as if its legs could no longer hold it upright. The people gave a great sigh, for in that moment, it looked like Esther would be triumphant against this darkness. But she too was a slave, and for a slave, triumph was far too fleeting. The creature raised a sinewy finger at Esther, and hope evaporated.

With a single gesture, the creature unleashed a column of flame upon Esther that swirled around until it engulfed her. Her primal shrieks rang out like an angelic horn and drove everyone back, falling to the ground. Everyone except Jacob.

"Mama!!!" he cried.

Without a second thought, he rushed to his mother's side. His small hands desperately tried to beat the flames back. But for every spot he doused, another flame would take its place. And the harder he fought, the brighter the flames grew.

Then, a clap of thunder boomed overhead and a finger of lightning struck at Jacob's feet. His child-like eyes suddenly became aglow. And the words his mother spoke, the language of his people, suddenly flowed from Jacob in a mature voice, not his own.

"Menifesini āsiralehu!!!" he shouted.

All at once, the flames receded from Esther and swirled around Jacob. But his skin remained unscathed as the fire danced from his fingertips. The fire obeyed the boy. Even the Inky Figure stood confused as Jacob gave it his full attention. He moved toward the Figure, stalking it like an angry wolf bearing upon its prey.

The Figure rose and lunged at Jacob, who stretched out his hand. The fire leapt from him and surrounded the Figure. It howled a ghastly scream as it fell back and slithered against a burning shack before writhing away into the night. Jacob called the flame back to him. It danced around his tiny hand before he shut his fist and snuffed it out.

"Mama!" he cried again.

He fell beside her and pulled her head against his tiny chest. The others finally came to their senses and brought blankets and water for Esther. Her hair singed, she gave Jacob a faint smile as she reached to touch his cheek. He focused on her, unfazed and unharmed. Except for a dark scar beneath his skin, as if the veins on one side of his face were seared by the lightning.

"My brave boy," she whispered.

Esther's gaze fell on her kinfolk, half expecting them to be looking upon her with hope and gratitude after coming through such an ordeal. But what she found was something that gave her as much pause as the creature they had defeated. After the long and brutal night, Esther found herself surrounded not by loving glances of relief, but by stares of profound and unimaginable fear... of Jacob.

Two

—··—

ARKANSAS, 1865

As the Civil War reached its twilight in history, slavery was not yet a footnote on the grave of the Confederacy. The dank stench of blood and gunpowder still hung heavy, like a ghost absent-minded about where it should go. The great South had long lost its sweet honeysuckle ambrosia. That scent had gone the way of the Choctaw that once roamed the plains in numbers beyond score. Long after the guns and cannons were silenced, the pungent malodor of death oozed from the ground. Borne of what remained of those hapless souls cut down well before they came into full season.

On a warm night in 1865, near the Arkansas border, the air was fragrant with the smell of wood burning from a small town in the distance. There was no moon in the night sky, and even the coyotes were eerily silent. Nothing, not even the crickets, made a sound. All was desolate, save the hooves of seven riders as they descended upon the town of Gilly Pines.

In its heyday, Gilly Pines was small but modestly impressive. Settled by two cousins who wanted a safe haven for their extended families, it had its boom time before becoming a home to other like-minded folks. A sturdy church, livery, and one of the cleanest saloons in three states. Somehow, the people of Gilly Pines were spared the ravages and brutality of the Civil War. But now black smoke blotted out the welcome post, and as it rose higher and higher, the smoke carried twinkling bright orange embers to the night sky.

With a sense of reverence and foreboding, the riders slowly entered the town. Their horses bristled and their voices clutched with fear as they discovered every building and structure burned to their foundation. Nothing, not even the battlefields that haunted some of their nightmares, compared to what they found. Some pulled up short and leaned over to retch violently at the sight of charred, dead bodies. Limbs were mangled, with a stinging stench that set their throats ablaze as they tried to navigate the desolate street.

"What in God's name happened here?" one rider asked.

"Maybe it was the savages!" another speculated. "What ya think, Sheriff?"

Leading the riders was Billup Poole, the Sheriff of Menifee, a neighboring town some twenty miles east of Gilly Pines. He was tall and wide-chested, with bloodshot eyes. Poole held a handkerchief over his mouth, occasionally dabbing at his eyes. He gripped the reins of his horse tight so as not to spook him. But it was Poole himself, spooked by the unspeakable sight before him.

"Sweet Jesus," he called out under his breath.

Poole steadied himself as his eyes fell on a woman, her charred arm stretched in his direction.

"Sheriff! There's more over here!" a rider called out.

The firelight glinted off Poole's badge as he wheeled his horse right toward the livery stable. He fought back the urge to dig his spurs into his horse and ride out as fast as it could carry him. But Poole knew something even his own men hadn't yet come to assess. This was the third town they'd found in such a state. And this one was too close to home.

Waiting for Poole at the livery stable was John Quail, Poole's lean and lanky deputy. All of twenty years old with the fear in his eyes of a man twice his age. Confusion marred his face, and his hands shook as he stared in utter shock. Quail wasn't built for this kind of brutal savagery the way Poole was and it showed.

"My God, they're all dead! All of them!" Quail exclaimed.

"Calm down, boy!" Poole hissed.

"Whole families in there!" Quail stammered. "What in God's name could do this?"

Poole didn't bother to answer as he dismounted and tied off his horse to a charred post. There was no answer that he could give so that the young deputy could wrap his mind around without pissing himself, and there was a good chance he still might. The sheriff grabbed his rifle and marched forward into the stable. Thankfully, the horses were nowhere in sight, but in their stalls... more bodies. Too many to count. Burned so badly, they fused one to the other, with no beginning and no end to them.

Poole reached out to touch an arm jutting from the pile as if to offer some comfort, but it turned to ash. To his left, the remains of a blacksmith sat upright like a statue and without a head. It took every ounce of strength Poole had not to vomit. Quail's shaky footsteps fell behind him.

"Sh-should we send for somebody? Maybe one of them Texas Rangers?" Quail asked.

Poole inched closer to the blacksmith. His eyes locked on an arrowhead at the man's feet. Against his better judgment, he reached for it. Suddenly, the stable creaked loudly. Boards whined as though the entire structure might give way over them. The sound lingered like the ghastly moan of a dying animal.

Poole stepped back. "Round up the rest of the men. Make sure they don't take a damn thing from here. This town's cursed."

"Sheriff?" Quail queried.

Poole turned to the frightened deputy with a steely gaze.

"Let it burn to the ground."

The deputy stood frozen as Poole marched out of the stable without another word. Quail had known this man since he could sit upright on a horse. He'd watched the sheriff single-handedly face down a gang of murderous marauders that threatened their town. He'd even seen him in a bare-knuckle fight with Mance Krueger, and win despite a broken arm. Quail had seen many faces on Billup Poole in his lifetime, but he had never witnessed fear on the man's face until this night. And the sight of it made him piss his pants where he stood.

THREE

It is said that the fireflies in Cincinnati, Ohio, can make the night sky appear as though the stars have fallen from heaven and make you feel the presence of God. But on this dark night at the Ketchum Farm, nothing but the cold moon blessed the sky. The moon loomed low, with a foreboding blood ring around it.

A horrific scream broke the stillness of the night and echoed across twelve acres. A young, freckle-faced boy ran with a lantern across the farm. He clutched a piece of cloth tight in his fist as he barreled toward a barn. He paused at the door, breathlessly taken aback. His eyes widened at the terrifying sight before him.

"Hurry, boy!" his father demanded.

Cautiously, the boy padded softly to his father, Earl Ketchum, a forty-year-old, second generation farmer, who was praying with all his heart he'd live to see a third. He struggled to hold on to the woman beneath him. Maggie Ketchum, his new bride, half his age. She was a sight to behold; blonde, beautiful, and spewing black bile as Earl tried to keep her at bay.

"Let me go, damn you! Let me go!" Maggie screamed like an animal, guttural-like.

The freckled boy ran to his three older siblings. Earl's children, all from his first wife, whimpered and held onto each other. As Earl's brother, and his brother's wife chanted prayers around Earl and Maggie, a large and imposing Black Man stood over them.

It was Jacob, now thirty years old, with a fractal lightning patterned scar on the side of his rugged face. His weathered countenance and tattered Union uniform weren't all that made him stand out. Jacob had grown a reputation over the years, one that made him feared and revered across the South. Soldier, Hero, Shaman, Healer. All culminated into a moniker whispered on the lips of white folks who had no one else to turn to when evil sat at their door: Black Bones Jones.

With a leather cord of charred human bones around his neck and a satchel at his side, he hovered over Maggie. He murmured in Amharic, his people's native tongue, powerful words beyond the simple understanding of the bewildered Ketchums. At the sight of the boy, he called out.

"Bring it here, child!" he bellowed.

Jones snatched the cloth from the boy and fastened it to Maggie's bosom with two blackened bones. Maggie growled like a rabid dog and cursed him aloud.

"Don't you touch me, darkie!" she snarled. "I'll send you back to the hell that birthed ya!"

Jones chanted, "Menifesini āsiralehu!"

He turned to the Ketchum clan, barking orders like a battle commander.

"Now all of you, hold her down!" Jones demanded.

The Ketchums quickly complied, laying their hands on Maggie. It took all of them to hold her to the ground as her back arched and she bucked against them.

"I'll kill ya! I'll kill all ya!" Maggie wailed.

Jones stood over her, taking a handful of ash from his satchel. He threw it over her.

"You'll kill no one while I'm here!" Jones fired back.

"I'll skin the black off of ya!" she replied viciously.

Jones reached forward, pressing a thumb of ash on the top of her head.

"I call you to be bound, unclean one," Jones shouted. "I call you to be bound now!"

Maggie screamed in a voice that was no longer her own. The Ketchum children ran to hide in a corner of the barn, only to find another stranger hiding there in the shadows. Sheriff Poole stared with awe and astonishment at this supernatural battle, his hands clasped around a cross.

Maggie's eyes rolled back as evil leapt from deep within her throat. "You help them? After they murdered your kin? Slaughtered them! Stole all they were and made them slaves!"

"You'll not seduce me the way you seduced this woman," Jones exclaimed. "I command you to speak your name and be drawn out!"

Earl and his brother fought to keep her arms pinned down as Maggie glared up at him.

"How can you 'llow that Black buck to lay hands on me? Your own wife!"

Jones glared hard at Earl. "Don't look into her eyes, lest the evil get into you too!"

Tears fell as Earl turned his head away and leaned in hard on Maggie. Jones knelt down over her, taking another handful of ash from his pocket. He pried open her mouth and poured some inside.

"By the blood, I call you out! By the name of above all names!" Jones shouted.

Maggie convulsed wildly and bucked beneath Jones like a stallion. More black bile spewed from her. Earl's sister-in-law shrieked and ran toward the barn.

"Maggie!" Earl cried.

"That's not your wife speaking. It's a spawn of hell itself!" Jones exclaimed.

Suddenly, Maggie's body rose from the ground, tossing Earl and his brother backward.

Only Jones could see what fate had spared the Ketchum family from witnessing. Black tendrils and blood-red eyes crept from behind Maggie's head. Tendrils that turned into demonic claws inching their way over her skin. This was what they were truly up against, not some creature of flesh and blood.

This was why Earl Ketchum's only hope was Black Bones Jones.

Jones held her face in his hands, chanting over and over again.

"Ganēni simihini nigerenyi! Ganēni simihini nigerenyi!"

But the venomous spirit inside of Maggie refused to be dispatched easily. Its tendrils dug their way into Jones's flesh as it coiled around her body with no beginning or end.

"I shall not fail, demon!" Jones raged.

It hissed back. "You'll see soon enough, Jacob Jones! You'll see your God won't protect you this time. Then we shall feast on your flesh!"

Unmoved by the demonic threats, Jones pressed harder, invoking all the power within him.

"Speak your name!" Jones demanded.

The tendrils retreated, only to be replaced by boils that erupted and coursed over Maggie's face. She writhed in pain as the ash ignited in her mouth. Her head snapped back and she let out a thunderous cry.

"Inisvaga! Inisvaga!" it hissed.

"Confess your name!" Jones commanded.

Sobbing, Maggie's demon could do nothing but relent. "INIS-VAGA!"

Clutching the bones on Maggie's chest, Jones summoned his mighty ancestral authority.

"Having confessed your name, I banish you back to the darkness!" He lifted the bones over Maggie's body. "Back from whence you came!"

The tendrils turned to ash and then smoke. The darkness streamed from Maggie's body, poured out in misty-colored flakes, and was sucked up into the bones around Jones's neck.

Maggie screamed. "Ahhhhhh!"

Free from the demon's grasp, Maggie fell to the barn floor as a spent Jones crumpled on top of her. For a moment, no one moved, and then Maggie coughed softly. Jones cradled her in his arms, brushing away the last of the ashen bile from her face. She was whole, restored to her young, vibrant self once more.

"Where, where am I?" Maggie stared all about, dazed.

Earl rushed to her side. Tears welled in his eyes as he pulled her into his arms.

"My sweet Maggie. Thank God!" he exclaimed.

Jones rose to his feet as Earl's brother rushed in, joyously, and the rest of the family came running from the safety of the barn. Maggie forced a smile, still not sure what had happened or why they blessed her with kisses. Jones gave them a hint of a smile.

Earl reached up to shake Jacob's hand. "By God, Mister, we owe you everything. How can I ever repay you?"

Jones politely took his hand. "Keepin' your word is a good start, Mr. Ketchum."

"On the eyes of my children, you'll have a wagon full and ready by morning, I swear it."

Suddenly all the Ketchums reached out for Jones as if drawing on him for strength and comfort. It was something that still made him uneasy, the embrace of people who once looked down on his ilk. But he was tolerant enough to allow them to show their appreciation.

"If it's alright, I'll make do in the barn for the night," Jones said. "You be with your family. Hold on to each other."

Earl nodded as Jones turned toward the shelter of the barn. With tears and thanksgiving in his eyes, Earl gathered Maggie up in his arms and carried her back to the main house.

Everyone followed except Sheriff Poole, who had witnessed the incredible encounter from a safe, respectable distance inside the barn.

Poole emerged shakily out of the shadows, lifting the brim of his hat to show his face. Jones regarded him with a sharp look and stepped toward a stall.

"Evening," Poole found his voice.

"Evening."

"That was mighty powerful to watch," Poole said, keeping a bit of space between them.

"If'n you're a bounty hunter, I got papers signed by the governor," Jones spoke. "You'd best move along."

Poole staggered left to peer at the spot where Maggie had nearly lost her life. The charred ground smoldered, yet there had been no bonfire.

"No sir. I'm Sheriff Poole out of Menifee," Poole informed him. "I take it I have the pleasure of addressing Mr. Jacob Jones?"

"Ain't nobody called me Jacob since I left Birmingham," Jones said. "And that's been some six years back now."

Poole pulled his hat from his head, clutching it against his chest.

"It's Black Bones Jones I find myself in the company of, then?"

Jones ambled to a blanket hung over a stall and laid it over the hay.

"Ain't never heard of Menifee," Jones replied. "Must be a mighty long way for a sheriff to come and watch me draw the darkness outta someone."

Poole shifted his feet across the ground. "Been tracking you for the last few days. Heard you were up near Columbus, just missed you by a day."

"I run afoul of the law somewhere, Sheriff?" Jones inquired. "I don't rightly recall ever having visited Menifee before."

Poole cleared his throat. "Right to it then. I respect that. We need your help. Something in my town — well, I don't right know how to describe it."

"Most folks don't. No shame in it." Jones wasn't making it easy for him.

"I take it you may have heard about the towns near the badlands, folks being beset by something unnatural, unspeakable," Poole explained. "Something they can't even say the Indians could have done."

"Heard some," Jones said. "Figured it was campfire tales to keep the children scared."

Poole stared hard at the black bile and soot on the ground. He turned away to hide the sudden urge to gag, recalling the burned bodies in Gilly Pines.

Jones removed his hat, then lay down on the blanket to settle in for the night.

Poole held his hat against his stomach and breathed slowly. "I've seen what it can do, Mr. Jones. Whole towns. Families. And I'm afraid it's coming to Menifee."

"Your being afraid means most likely it's already headin' there," Jones responded.

Poole turned to him, annoyed Jones seemed so indifferent.

"I'm trying to save my town, Mr. Jones," he pleaded. "I've come with hat in hand, asking for your help."

Jones sat upright, staring at Poole for a beat. He took in his stature, tall and determined, behind his shiny badge. There was a strange humility behind his mask of pride, like a man struggling to keep his head above water, and Poole was drowning. But Jones wasn't a man inclined in that moment to lessen the load for him.

"Not easy for you, is it?" Jones asked. "Coming to a man you'd soon as take a whip to or see him rot in a field — with hat in hand, as you say?"

"A Slaver? That's how you take my request?" Poole sneered.

"Not rightly sure yet how to take you, Sheriff," Jones responded.

"Maybe I'm not speaking plainly. I need your help. I mean to have it," Poole replied.

Jones watched as Poole's hand fell on the gun at his side. He met Poole's eyes with a stony gaze, completely surprised to find desperation and not the arrogance he expected.

"Plain enough," Jones said. "Sheriff. Plain enough."

"So, will you help us?" Poole asked.

"Might you be persuaded to leave me a map to Menifee," Jones asked. "Say I could make it there in a week's time?"

"Thinking it's better we travel together," Poole forced a smile. "You might even find the company hospitable."

Jones eyed him darkly as he rubbed ash from his hands. Trust was something that didn't come easy for him and for good reason. Many a time men had come searching for him, claiming to seek his help, only to have their true intentions revealed and at the cost of their lives.

"If I might be equally plain, Sheriff," Jones glared. "You might reconsider, given what you've seen me do and how it affects folks. My work has some remnants that you ain't yet been acquainted with yet. Things that linger long after. Few men got the stomach for it."

A rustling in the darkness drew their attention. Poole drew his gun and pivoted, as Jones tracked his gaze.

"Just field mice," Poole decided, putting his gun back.

Jones rose to his feet. Walking toward the darkness, he drew a match from his pocket.

"Maybe." Jones lit the match, then held it up to the dark. "Maybe not."

The flickering light revealed a Mangled Creature, twisted and black, like a dozen serpents coiled over a faceless torso. It fell away from the light with a hiss and slithered into the darkness that birthed it.

"Jesus!" Poole stumbled and fell back on his ass.

"You alright, Sheriff Poole?" Jones blew out the match.

Poole swallowed hard and scurried back to his feet. His eyes cut back at Jones, watching him caress the bones around his neck.

"Wh-what in God's name was that?" Poole stammered.

Jones regarded the dark corner with a careless shrug. "Shadows got a way of playing on a man's fears. Make him see and hear things he ought not. But as I said, my work has some remnants."

Poole grimaced but didn't argue. "All the same, just as well we ride together. If you're agreeable?"

Jones countered. "How 'bout we discuss it over breakfast, Sheriff? I'm always more agreeable on a full stomach."

Jones heaved a heavy sigh and gave him a long dark glare. He walked to the barn door and shut it tightly, locking them in. The full moon shone through the only window, casting long shadows across the barn floor.

"Fair enough, Mr. Jones." Poole stared long into the darkness, waiting for his eyes to adjust to the low light.

"Good sleep'll help us both." Jones returned to his spot, nestled in, and closed his eyes.

Reasonably satisfied with Jones's acceptance, Poole lumbered to a nearby stall and settled in. He kept his gun close at hand. His eyes remained fixed on the dark corner. A faint growl from the darkness would keep him awake until dawn.

***

A weary-eyed Poole watched as the Ketchums bid Jones a grateful farewell. Something about it made him uneasy, the way they fawned over him like a distant cousin recently returned from an extended absence. It was more than just not being accustomed to seeing white people show such kindness toward a colored man. It was personal. Poole had never known that kind of affection in his whole life. Not even from his mother or father. No one ever gave him the kind of grace he bore witness to at that moment. A part of Poole envied Jones, who shifted nervously while the Ketchums hugged and thanked him.

The days ahead of them would be arduous and long. If the journey went as planned, they'd cross the Ohio River and make camp in Kentucky on the third night. Fortunately for them both, Earl Ketchum made sure they were well-supplied, more so for Jones than Poole. His nomadic lifestyle saved him the indignities of unfriendly towns or folks still bitter from how the war had turned out. It wasn't the best life, but it was what he alone chose, and for Jones, that meant everything.

As Jones approached the wagon, he felt Poole's eyes on him. He adjusted his trousers, reached into the wagon for his gun belt, and wrapped it around his waist. From the wagon, he hoisted two howdah pistols with long, black double barrels, and holstered them at his sides. Poole took note of the strange symbols inscribed in the polished wood handles, likely only decipherable by Jones. A remnant from the war and battles he'd rather soon forget.

Jones climbed onto the seat of the wagon, picking up the reins.

"Reckon you ready to get started, Sheriff?" he asked.

"You reckon right."

With a melancholy frown, Poole mounted his horse, and they headed out.

FOUR

With the sunrise at their backs, Jones chose a well-worn, westbound wagon trail. For the better part of an hour, he silently manned the wagon, and Poole rode astride, eyeing the supplies stacked high in the wagon. Dry goods, blankets, baskets of vegetables, cured meat, and a salt lick. More than a man needs.

"You planning a party?" Poole inquired.

"Barter some. Mexico for the rest."

Curious, Poole asked, "You got people there?"

Jones gripped the reins tighter, hesitant to answer. "Some."

Poole noted the tension in his voice. Jones' Union uniform and hat had seen better days.

"I fought for the North too," Poole admitted.

Jones nodded, but offered nothing so Poole tried a different angle.

"You a Christian man, Jones?"

"In what way?"

Poole shrugged. "I don't know. I never put much stock in it. Believing in God, following Jesus and whatnot."

Jones sighed, "Can I ask you a question, Sheriff?"

"Course."

"Seeing as how every story in the Bible comes from the place of my people, how do you reckon your people think they know God better than mine?" Jones asked.

It was a question that cast a look of worry over Poole's face.

"My people have known God long before your kind came to us," Jones explained. "We just understand God in a different way."

"How's that?" Jones considered this. "White people's religion is all about what you gotta do. Our faith is in what's already been done. It's stronger."

"Yeah, but didn't He allow your people to become slaves?" Poole wondered aloud.

"Did God tell your people to enslave us, or did you come to that of your own accord?"

Something about the question rubbed Poole the wrong way. It made him squirm in his saddle. He struggled to answer. "Like I said, I don't put much stock in God or the devil."

Jones smiled. "And yet you sought me out."

"I guess what I saw in the war..." Poole's eyes drifted off. "Let's say it gave me pause."

Jones eyed him with understanding. "You can't have seen war and not believe in both."

"That how you come by your calling?" Poole asked.

Jones chewed on it for a moment, glancing down at his hands. Old scars from the lash of a whip snaked up his arms.

"Way, I see it, Lord don't always call. Sometimes He just plucks you out of the darkness and lays His hands on you. Don't mean what you're given gon' make life easy. In fact, it's a burden. But you carry it because you were chosen."

"So, God gave you power over devils?" Poole asked.

Jones gave Poole an icy glare, fueled by a life defined by brutality and unimaginable sorrow. His mind raced back beyond the war-torn battlefields, beyond beatings, to losing his family on a fateful night. The Dark Figure still haunted his dreams.

"Depends on who or what you call the devil."

***

With the midday sun high above, Jones stretched his legs near the wagon, while Poole squatted somewhere in the wooded area nearby. At this pace, Poole's frequent stops to visit the woods would add at least an extra day to their journey, and Jones was feeling impatient. After checking his horse over, he searched the wagon for something to eat. Jones bit down hard into an over-ripe black tomato, wiping the dark purple juice with his arm. Poole returned from the woods and wiped his hands on some leaves. Seeing Jones eating, Poole found comfort in a stick of dried meat he'd tucked away in his saddle, and offered some to Jones.

"Might go down a bit better than that tomato," he encouraged Jones.

"Ain't never quite had the stomach for cured meat," Jones declined.

Poole bit off a hunk. "Good to keep a man full on a ride like this."

"Appreciate it all the same," Jones replied.

Poole eyed Jones as he chewed, not quite able to read his mood.

"Might I ask a question?" Poole inquired. "You a preacher's son?"

"Wasn't raised to be a son of a preacher."

"You take after some white holy man?" Poole asked, mounting his horse.

Jones finished his tomato with a bit of a glare in Poole's direction. "You think a white man taught me what I know?"

Poole shrugged. "Maybe you were like an apprentice, I figure."

"What I know, no white man ever knew," Jones explained, getting back on the wagon. "Let alone see fit to teach somebody like me."

Jones signaled his horses to pull the wagon again. Poole rode up alongside, sensing he had misspoken.

"Wasn't no offense meant by it. I'm just curious as to how this became your life. Ain't never heard of anyone like you before. Colored man curing white folk of these things."

The tension in Jones' demeanor softened. He let out a heavy sigh.

"Can't say I'm the first like me and reckon I won't be the last," Jones explained. "I don't just do it for white folks. Just folks in need. It ain't the kind of thing my people speak of openly. But it goes back to the time before we found ourselves in this land."

"Guess negro folk got their own kind of magic, huh?" Poole asked.

"Magic?" Jones chuckled. "Ever ask yourself how it comes to pass that the Lord and Savior look more like a man from Europe than a man from Africa? Egypt, Bethlehem, all of them places cradled in the heart of the so-called dark continent, but people believe the Son of God was a white man?"

Poole pondered this. "I can't say I ever seen it like that."

"All faith and religion came from one place," Jones said. "And if'n you believe it so, that also means we're more kin than you realize."

For Poole, this thought was quite unsettling, yet it stirred up a long-buried curiosity. As a young man, he dared only once to ask questions about his family's ownership of slaves, and was swiftly met with the back of his father's hand. Spare the rod was never his family's practice, especially when it came to questioning the station of slaves.

Defeated, Poole replied, "I was just wanting to know is all."

"Like all men, I am both blessed and cursed, Sheriff," Jones lamented. "I am what I'm meant to be. My calling is to root out the darkness in folks. And as often as I come across it, I wouldn't wish on any man the darkness on my path."

It was Poole now whose eyes softened, somehow feeling the weight of the burden Jones carried, and though he didn't fully understand it, he thanked God under his breath, that such a thing should never find its way into his life.

***

On the fourth day, they made it across the Ohio River and set up camp on the outskirts of the deep Kentucky woods just before nightfall. The wind blew through the red cedars and made a low moaning sound like an off-key choir in the dead of night. The kind of thing that made a man sleep lightly or not at all. Poole started a fire as Jones grabbed a large sack from the wagon and marched a few yards away. When he'd gone far enough, Jones began pouring salt onto the ground, making a circle around the whole of the camp, wagon and horses included. He muttered his mother's language under his breath until he ended where he began, careful to keep his feet inside the circle.

As he marched back to the wagon, Poole called out, "Whatcha doin that for?"

"Protection," Jones replied.

Poole's eyes scanned the edge of the woods. He scratched his head.

"What we need protection from?"

Jones secured the sack back in the wagon, then padded slowly back to the fire. He knelt down, staring into the flames.

"You still ain't pieced it together yet, Sheriff?" Jones asked. "There's a world of things under heaven that few men understand. Things like what you saw in Ketchum's barn back in Ohio."

"How you know what I saw?" Poole fired back.

Jones picked up a few twigs to throw in the fire, then sat on the ground.

"When I was young, I heard tales of men and women going into the woods at night and ain't nobody ever hear from them again," Jones started.

A chill went up Poole's spine, and his eyes widened.

Jones poked at the fire and continued. "Now there come a time when my army regiment spent the night in woods like these. White soldiers slept close to the trees. Black soldiers stayed in the open."

Jones eased down on one arm as Poole stared at him.

"Every now and then, we hear something. A branch snapping or leaves rustling, but it's too dark to see," Jones said. "Sarge told us it ain't nothing and just get some sleep. Come morning, some of them white soldiers wasn't there."

"Where'd they go?" Poole asked.

Jones shook his head. "Ain't nobody know at first. Later we found one of them."

Jones sat upright for what came next.

"We found him flailed like a side of beef," Jones recalled. "His skin was stretched up high in the trees. And his insides were carved out clean to the bone. I've seen a man scalped, but ain't no Redman I know ever do that."

Poole bristled, trying to hide his fear. "M-must have been some kind of animal."

"What animal you know can drag five men off without making a sound?" Jones asked.

Poole didn't have an answer. Truth be told, he didn't want to know. Jones had opened his eyes to things he could barely wrap his mind around. Although he'd never spent this much time in such close proximity to a Black man, this went beyond the color of Jones' skin. This shook the very foundation of the man. Jones stood up, hurried back to the wagon, and then returned with a pair of blankets and his guns. He tossed a blanket over to Poole, who immediately wrapped himself, likely more for the feeling of safety than for warmth.

"As long as we stay in the circle, no harm come to us," Jones stated.

Poole nodded, bewildered. Jones folded his blanket under his head and laid his guns next to him.

"Ain't you gon' say your prayers or something?" Poole asked.

"I pray with every breath I take, Sheriff," Jones replied.

"Must be a colored thing," Poole grumbled.

"Then I reckon you wouldn't understand." Jones closed his eyes.

Much later in the night, Poole tossed and turned, barely able to quiet his mind. His thoughts raced wildly. He feared the destruction that was heading for his town. Would they arrive in time? He grappled with what he'd experienced since he met Jones. What was in the dark corner of the barn? Did it follow them? All of it tormented him. He hadn't dared to empty his bladder before bedding down, but he couldn't hold it anymore. He rose from the ground and stumbled toward a tree at the edge of the circle. Sleep-deprived and saddle-weary, he didn't notice that one of his boots broke the line of salt. Sufficiently relieved, Poole yawned and walked back to his blanket to once again attempt to sleep. As the night drew on, neither man was immediately aware of the shadows moving about them, skulking just outside the circle in eerie whispers.

They were called Buulagg, as dark as the night. They stood no higher than a child, half-grown with pointed fingers. These were the denizens of the woods, neither indigenous nor slave, the discarded and forgotten among white men who saw no value in their existence. But in the shadows among the trees, something dark and twisted welcomed them and bestowed unto them unholy gifts. Poole snored, as the Buulagg huddled near the spot where he'd broken the circle, childishly chiding each other, and pointing in his direction. One of them pushed another into the circle, surprised nothing happened to it. Another jumped beside the first and then the others joined in. Poole lay oblivious as they huddled around him, their tiny fingers poking him with the slightest touch. They conspired in whispers above his body before they finally grabbed his legs and slowly started pulling him away.

One of them broke ranks and made its way toward Jones. It sniffed over him, eyeing Jones curiously and raised its hand over his head. As they neared the edge of the circle, one of them kicked up a loose pebble which bounced off of Poole's face and startled him awake.

"What in tarnation?!"

The Buulagg hissed at him through tiny sharp teeth as they dug their fingers into him.

"Jones!" Poole screamed, struggling to free himself.

Jones opened his eyes to see the Buulagg standing over him. Jones spun himself backward, narrowly avoiding its swipe. It hissed and reared back on its haunches, preparing to strike. Jones rolled onto his stomach, grasped the handle of one of his guns, and raised it.

"Not today," Jones told it.

He fired and threw the Buulagg twenty feet in the air, shrieking. It came crashing to the ground with a hole in its chest the size of a man's head. Poole gawked at the carcass, then at Jones, bewildered. The other Buulagg scrambled, putting themselves between Jones and Poole, like ravenous animals desperate to hold on to their prey.

"Jones!" Poole screamed again. Jones reached for his satchel and sprung to his feet, keeping the gun pointed at them.

"Poole!" Jones called out. "Whatever you do, don't let them drag you outside the circle!"

"Do something, Jones!" Poole shouted. "Don't let 'em take me!"

One of the Buulagg turned back to Poole. Its eyes grew larger, glowing a hellish green. It opened its maw and bellowed like a wild boar. Momentarily free of the grasp of the Buulagg, Poole wailed, pushing away toward the edge of the circle. He halted when he felt the salt ring against his fingers.

"Poole!" Jones screamed. "Shut your eyes and don't move!"

As the Buulagg closed in on them, Jones sidestepped to his other pistol, still on the ground. In rapid motion, he slid the toe of his boot under it and flipped it up into his free hand. Holding both guns in one hand, he reached into his satchel to scoop out a handful of ash, then quickly sifted it into the barrels of both pistols. He tramped up to the line of Buulagg, guns in each hand. Thunder crashed overhead.

"Leave now or by God, I'll send you straight to hell!" Jones proclaimed.

The Buulagg hissed in defiance. Jones pointed his pistols in two directions, attempting to cover all of them. He fired one. The ash ignited, creating a cloud of fire that swept the front line and burned everything it touched. Buulagg screeched and scattered, trying to douse the flames. Jones aimed the second double barrel at the ones bold enough to hold their ground. He fired another burst into their midst, spraying fire across them. Some writhed on the ground, and some leapt over Poole, trying to escape the flames. Jones marched up to the closest one and stomped on its head, crushing it like peanuts under his heel. In moments, he was standing over Poole, pivoting his guns back and forth as they scattered into the night.

"Get up," Jones holstered one of his pistols.

Poole opened his eyes to see Jones above him, holding out his hand.

"Thank God!" Poole exclaimed. "I thought I was—"

"—Ain't over yet," Jones cut him off.

Jones stepped ahead of Poole to the edge of the circle. He reloaded ash into his guns and waited.

"Jesus," Poole said. "What are you—"

"—Shut up," Jones demanded. "It's coming."

"W-what?" Poole stammered.

A howl erupted from deep in the woods. Jones aimed his guns directly ahead of them. Silence. Suddenly, the sound of a thunderous stampede filled the night. As it drew closer, Poole fell back, cowering. Jones braced himself for whatever was coming. Then out of the woods emerged a hulking Buulagg female the size of a grizzly. Its heaving breasts swung as it barreled toward them. This was the mother, and it was angry.

"Shoot it, Jones!" Poole exclaimed.

But Jones waited for it to draw closer.

"What the hell are you waiting for?" Poole cried out. "Shoot it!"

Again, Jones remained still, as it narrowed the space between them.

"Shoot!" Poole screamed.

When it was almost on top of Jones, he fired both guns, blasting half of its face away and blowing a hole in its chest. With a quiet swoosh, it fell at Jones' feet, twitching and gurgling until it was dead.

"Jesus," Poole exhaled in relief.

Jones whirled back to Poole with rage in his eyes. Poole tried to back away, but Jones grabbed him by the collar.

"How the fuck did they get inside the circle?" Jones demanded.

"What?"

"Did you break the damn circle?" Jones shouted.

Poole paled. He gulped, struggling for words.

"I j-just... I-I had to pee."

Jones sighed, releasing his grip. Nothing he could do would scare Poole any more than what they'd just survived. Jones shook his head and stomped over to the wagon.

"Jones, I'm sorry," Poole apologized.

"We need to go," Jones said.

"What? Why?" Poole asked.

Jones spun back at Poole again.

"The circle's broken. There's more of them out there and they'll be coming back."

"B-but can't we just make another circle?"

"Don't work that way," Jones explained, as he grabbed his blanket. "Breaking the circle is like an invitation. No tellin' how many of them Buulagg's still out there and I ain't waitin' around to find out."

Poole followed him back to the wagon, barely able to comprehend what had happened.

"Maybe you scared them off," Poole wondered aloud. "Maybe they—"

Poole stopped short as he came face-to-face with Jones' glare. It was a dark, foreboding grimace that, for a moment, made Jones look anything but human.

"Best I explain what woulda happened if I let them take you," Jones began. "First all of they woulda skinned you slowly, taking turns making sure they all get a taste. Then they'd cut chunks of you off to eat. While you're screaming and hollerin', they'd pull you apart and gnash you to the bone. Whatever's left over, they gon' cover themselves in."

Poole swallowed hard, "Christ."

"Now load up," Jones ordered. "I give 'em an hour 'til they get the nerve to come back."

Jones started gathering their things from the ground. Poole shook his head in disbelief.

"How do you do this, Jones?" Poole stammered. "How do you see it all and not go crazy?"

Jones shrugged, tossing the last of their things into the back of the wagon. He turned to Poole, noting the fear in his eyes.

"Who knows?" Jones replied. "Maybe it's a Black thing."

FIVE

_—·—_

They made up most of their lost time, putting as much distance between them and the horrific night in Kentucky. They reached the Tennessee border in a week, keeping conversation about the trail and the weather, mostly. Poole was too afraid to ask any more questions, and he didn't quite know how to explain what he'd witnessed in Gilly Pines, so he stayed pretty quiet—except for his frequent indigestion. Jones did his best to focus his thoughts on what lay ahead and tried to ignore Poole's somewhat intrusive bodily functions. They stuck to the well-traveled wagon trail, happening upon the occasional picked over animal carcass or remnants of a former campsite, but not much else.

Deep in Tennessee, they made camp just before nightfall. Jones stirred beans over a fire. Poole was off relieving himself near some tall bushes, far enough away for privacy, but nowhere near the shadows of the woods. Jones took a hunk of dried meat from his pocket and frowned at it. Decidedly too hungry to be finicky, he took a bite and stared deep into the fire. Something about the orange-red flames brought a distant memory to the surface. His thoughts carried him back to another time when he was much younger.

***

An eighteen-year-old Jones, nowhere near the stoic figure he is now, stood anxious and bare-chested before a group of slaves who'd hidden themselves in the woods. They chanted in Amharic as they guided him to an open fire. This was more than a ritual — it was their faith. Some danced as their ancestors had danced a thousand years ago. Others stood watch to make sure none of the overseers or anyone from the main house caught a glimpse of them.

Jones exhaled, nervous but ready. Two women chanted as they led an Elder man wrapped in a blanket to the scene. His eyes were sullen yet kind as he raised them to gaze at Jones. He dropped the blanket, revealing he had one arm and a string of charred bones around his neck.

"As my father and his father..." the Elder man began, "... and his father before him, I call upon the Guardians who gave the sacred words passed from generations."

He lifted the bones from his neck and held them over the fire. The flames did him no harm.

"Now comes the time of passing," the Elder announced.

The flames grew higher. The Elder nodded. Jones reached in. His skin singed until he grasped the Elder's hand.

The people all chanted, "To our ancestors we give thanks."

"To our ancestors, we give thanks," Jones repeated.

Jones struggled to keep his eyes on the Elder and not his own hand.

The Elder smiled at Jacob. "This gift I give with their blessing." He twisted his wrist and let the bones dangle over Jones's hand.

"This gift I accept with their blessing," Jones replied.

The Elder smiled as his hand suddenly withered. He clamped his fist over Jones' hand and turned to the women. One of them raised a hatchet and chopped his hand off. The blackened bones fell into Jones's hand. The other woman turned the Elder toward her to tend his wound. With a smile of finality, he nodded at Jones before the woman led the Elder away. The remaining woman set down the hatchet. She took the string of bones from around Jones's hand and lifted the necklace. He prayerfully cast his eyes downward. Then, she whispered words in their Mother tongue and placed the bones around his neck.

The people sang, "Praise the gift, born of the light. Behold the keeper of the night."

They crowded around Jones and whisked him away into the shadows.

***

Jones, lost in the memory of that long ago night, hummed the same ancestral song to himself. A branch crackled, alerting Jones back to the present. His ears pricked at a second snap, which came from the opposite of Poole's direction. Jones stopped stirring the fire. He reached for his side. His eyes widened. His gun belt was twenty paces away, hanging over the wagon. Horses neighed, and the crackling grew into hard hooves, drawing closer before Jones had time to move.

He grabbed a dried hunk of bark as nine riders emerged from the woods. They were Slavers, men who made their living by illegally capturing freed people, even now, more than two years since the Emancipation Proclamation and several months since the Confederacy fell. They returned their captors to well-hidden plantations for a lucrative bounty, especially for a man the size of Jones. The first rider, Collins, who wore a hardened grimace and a graying beard, rode hard into camp. He pulled up short, just in front of the fire. His men surrounded Jones, their guns drawn. Heavy chains and shackles hung forebodingly over their saddles.

"The hell do we have here, boys?" Collins mused. "Some darkie alone in the night?"

Jones dared not risk speaking, but he met Collins's gaze.

"What you doing out here, boy?" Collins glared.

Jones swallowed hard as Collins dismounted and scanned the area. He signaled one of his men to check the wagon. The man dismounted, sauntered over to the wagon, and climbed in.

"You deaf, boy?" Collins barked with a grin.

Jones eased the bark back onto the ground. Against such numbers, he had little chance. He might fare better if he appeared unarmed.

"And wearing Yankee clothes? You steal 'em or you fight with 'em?"

Jones glared hard, readying himself. Even his satchel was out of reach.

"Ain't no matter. We'll have you back where you belong soon enough," Collins grinned.

One of Collins's men called out. "No one else here, Boss."

Collins squatted low and smiled at Jones.

"You a big buck, I'll give ya that. I imagine you'll fetch a right good sum for somebody."

One of Collins' men tossed his chains next to Jones.

"So boy, we gon' do this the easy way or the hard way?" Collins taunted.

"That ought to be a question you should be asking me, Mister," Poole called out from the tree line.

They all turned to see Poole, his shotgun raised high and aimed at Collins.

"You'll be good enough to step away from my property," Poole demanded.

The other seven men drew their guns. The goon in the wagon froze. Collins raised his hands slowly, still eyeing Jones.

"Hold on now. We had no idea he belonged to anyone."

The man on the wagon eased himself back to the ground, keeping his eyes on Poole's gun.

"We ain't mean no harm, Mister."

Poole tilted his badge, so it glimmered off the firelight.

"That depends on if none of my belongings are missing. You boys regularly go around robbing folks?"

Collins rose and humbly removed his hat, meeting Poole's gaze.

"We ain't no robbers, Sheriff."

Upon hearing Collins say 'sheriff,' the other seven gunmen quickly put their guns away and raised their hands up.

"Sheriff, we're good men doing honest work," Collins said, suddenly without his gang's protection.

"Then you'll have no problem getting back on your horses and moving on."

The man near the wagon hurried over to mount his horse, but Collins' greedy eyes drifted back to Jones, who still hadn't said a word.

"You sure you ain't of a mind to sell him? Offer you a good price. Some places still pay good, no matter what Lincoln did," Collins pushed.

Poole racked his shotgun with defiant authority.

"Can't say I'm in a selling mood."

"Gotta say you ain't at all being neighborly, Sheriff." Collins rubbed his chin.

Poole stepped closer and trained his gun on Collins's head.

"Suppose I come into your camp and start rummaging through your things and threaten to take your property? I expect I'd be staring down the barrel of a gun as you are now."

Collins gave him a pained nod, his eyes crossing at the tip of the gun.

"Can't rightly argue that."

"Get over here, boy," Poole called out to Jones.

Jones cut his eyes at Poole, the shock of it almost finding its way to his mouth before he choked it back down. Collins watched curiously from behind Poole's barrel as Jones sat frozen.

"You hear me, boy?" Poole shouted.

Jones got up and lumbered his way to Poole's side. Poole kept his gun on Collins and swept his boot across the back of Jones's calves, buckling him down onto hands and knees. Jones dug his fingers into the earth to remain hunched over. He gritted his teeth to keep his head hung low. Satisfied, Collins put his hat back on his head and raised his hands.

"Deeply sorry for any trouble, Sheriff. We'll be on our way," Collins swiftly jumped back on his horse. "Come on, boys."

Collins signaled his horse into action, and his posse followed him, looking over their shoulders while Poole kept his gun on them. Once he was satisfied that they had faded back into the night, Poole slowly lowered his gun.

"Sweet Jesus." Poole heaved a heavy sigh. "You alright?"

Jones stood in a furious rage. He punched Poole hard in the face, knocking him on his ass. Jones stood over him, seething.

"Ain't no man call me boy and live to talk the 'morrow! I ain't your boy!"

Poole sat there for a moment, stunned by Jones' ferocity.

"I had to — I didn't see no other way," Poole pushed himself up to his knees as he nursed his jaw. "I ain't gonna lie to ya. I came up with slaves, but I don't care much for it. I didn't have a choice — they were gonna take you and you're the only hope for my people. I couldn't risk losing you."

Jones stepped back, chest heaving as he turned to face the fire.

"I ain't nobody's boy."

Poole stood and brushed himself off. He stared at Jones, maudlin.

"I ain't no saint, but I can't be held guilty for other men's crimes, Jones."

"Ain't on me to condemn you, Sheriff," Jones headed for the wagon. "Ain't on me to forgive you either," he grumbled under his breath.

A hundred years of pain and suffering opened between them. The Civil War had ended months ago, but the wounds between Black and White, rich and poor, North and South—those would remain for generations upon generations.

At that moment, a warm wind blew into the camp. Sheriff Billup Poole suddenly felt overcome with an ache in the pit of his soul, like he had never known before. It was a deep, painful awareness that could profoundly change a man forever. As he watched Jones climb into the wagon, Poole caught a fleeting glimpse of what it was like to live in a world that hated you for no good reason at all. The wind picked up, swirled past Poole and extinguished the fire.

***

It was just outside of Memphis that fate dealt them a blow. As Poole swept to his left, descending a steep hill, his horse stutter-stepped on a loose rock and threw him.

"Fuck!" Poole screamed as he hung awkwardly off the side of his horse. Jones fought back the urge to laugh. Poole managed to dismount and check his horse's leg.

Poole grimly examined his horse. "It's not bad, but he'll be limp the rest of the way."

"Best tie him off and climb on," Jones suggested.

Poole realized heeding Jones' advice made sense. "Yeah, I guess so," he groaned.

He tied his horse to the wagon as Jones offered him a hand. With the better part of two weeks on the trail behind them, neither man was fit for close conversation on a wagon seat. In part, it was their sun-baked body odor, but mostly it was the knowledge of the darkness they'd already encountered and the fear of what might be waiting for them in Arkansas. For nearly four more days, neither offered more than a grunt now and then, all the way to Menifee.

Six

Menifee, Arkansas

Fifty years ago, Menifee was a boomtown, a sparkling jewel for idealistic families looking for a fresh start in the new land. Settled by men of sturdy stock, it thrived on being a passage of comfort for those heading west. But the decline of trailblazers, followed by the war, took a heavy toll that left the once vibrant town as lackluster as the dusty roads that led to it. Now, with its worn and weathered, half-century-old buildings, Menifee was a town barely clinging to life, like a wounded animal that didn't have the good sense to lie down and die.

Jones and Poole arrived late in the day under darkening skies and a cold wind that shifted between the scent of pine lofting from the saloon and the stench that wafted from an outhouse nearby. Poole sat next to Jones as the wagon made its way down to the main street, teetering over small holes in the dusty road.

It didn't take townsfolk long to notice their sheriff seated next to a colored man, not that it was an unusual occurrence, but Jones held his head higher than most. Like a man who believed he had every right to meet the ominous gazes of those who once would have cruelly admonished him for such a thing. He held their gaze until each man and woman looked away in confusion and doubt. It brought Jones the faintest hint of a smile.

Parson Greene, a gangly man of thirty years, stepped into their path. His white, stiff collar fit oddly around his long neck, a little too loose in some spots and too tight in others.

With a smile as wide as the Red Sea, he called out, "The Lord be with you, Sheriff. Who is this wretched soul you've rescued with you?"

"This man is here to help," Poole responded.

"Him?" Greene looked Jones up and down with both an air of disdain and disbelief.

"The name's Jones, Mister," Jones replied.

"It's Parson, sir," Greene fired back. "I would've thought even your kind would recognize a man of God."

"Oh, I recognize and heed the good book more than you know, Parson," Jones met the minister's eyes. "And I ain't afraid of the pestilence that walketh in darkness."

Greene stood there with his mouth agape, stunned by Jones' response.

"What?" Greene questioned.

"Psalm 91, Parson," Jones explained. "Figured you'd know that."

Poole coughed aloud to hide a chuckle at Jones putting Greene in his place.

"Best be on our way, Jones," Poole said.

"None but the Good Lord will save the good folks of Menifee!" Greene stated loudly.

"Reckon we will see, Parson." Poole clicked the horses to continue.

Hopping out of the way, Greene remarked, "We shall indeed, Sheriff!"

Jones noted the looks exchanged between Poole and the pastor. It was clear neither of them were in each other's prayers.

"Friend of yours?" Jones asked.

"Not since I married his sister," Poole replied, hiding a smirk.

More people emerged from each building they passed, some darkly so.

"Friendly I see," Jones surmised.

"They're used to things being a certain way," Poole stated. "Ain't easy since the war."

"Change is hard for some folks," agreed Jones.

Poole nodded sheepishly, glaring back at some of his residents. "I'm just asking you to hold any judgement regarding their temperament. Most are just scared."

Jones remained unwavering, as a group of women whispered and pointed at him. A man next to the women laid his hand on his gun.

"They ain't all afraid," Jones said.

Poole clocked his gaze to the man and sighs. "They ain't all smart either."

Jones chuckled. Poole laughed out loud.

As Jones guided the wagon before the Sheriff's office, an elderly resident crossed their path. Willa Stanton seemed frail but was quite spry despite her 80 years. Her faded frock, once the talk of the town for its expensive beauty, now garnered a different kind of talk, as it hung oddly on her like a young girl in her mother's old ball gown. She paused, eyeing them with great interest as they came to a stop. She smiled as Poole tipped his hat to her.

"Morning, Widow Stanton," Poole greeted her.

"Good morning, Sheriff Poole." Her smile was accentuated by the lines on her face. But even time couldn't dim her glow. Her eyes narrowed on Jones. "They've been expecting you, child."

Jones returned a polite smile.

"They told me a Black buck was coming to save the town, but I don't put much stock in gossip," she explained.

"Sounds like wise advice, ma'am," Jones answered.

Her eyes sparkled with curiosity as she sized up Jones.

"So much sadness in your eyes. I expect that's always been your way."

Poole shifted uncomfortably, trying to measure a response to the widow's odd statement.

"I expect so," Jones stated darkly.

Poole feigned a cough and then said, "Best we get to our business then. All the best to you, Widow Stanton."

"They'll all be grateful for you," Willa proclaimed. "They told me, so it must be true."

Poole shrugged at Jones. Willa crossed the street behind them, headed toward the mercantile.

"Pay her no heed. Her mind ain't been right for a good spell now," Poole explained.

Jones glanced back over his shoulder, only to find her staring at them. She stood frozen, as if the very ground beneath her forbade her to leave. But her lips moved ever so slightly, and Jones could see her whispering some voiceless oration meant only for her ears. Then, as if awakened from a dream, she smiled, turned, and went on her way into the shop.

"I'll take your word for it," Jones sighed.

***

Inside the sheriff's office, Deputy Quail waxed the day away, feet propped up on Poole's desk, while chewing on a hint of straw. The sound of the door opening made him nearly jump out of his skin. He fumbled his way to his feet, doing his best to put on a dignified air of authority. It faded all too soon at the sight of Jones behind Poole.

"Sheriff," he greeted. "This the man you've been looking for?"

Poole gestured in Quail's direction. "My deputy, Quail. This here is Mister Jones."

Deputy Quail extended his hand to Jones, who was taken aback by the gesture.

"Pleased to make your acquaintance," Quail said with a smile.

Jones shook his hand warmly. "Much obliged, Deputy Quail."

He watched as Quail studied him from head to toe. The wonder and fear behind the deputy's eyes were all too apparent, and all too familiar. At least with Quail, it seemed there was far less judgment in his stare.

"I've heard stories about your—what do you call what you do?" Quail asked.

"Some days, a gift. Some days, a curse. Most days, not much," Jones replied.

Quail chuckled heartily until he felt Poole's eyes burning into him.

"Things've been pretty quiet since you left, Sheriff," Quail reported. "But some folks already pulled up stakes."

Jones' eyes narrowed on Quail. "Something happen?"

Quail's eyes darted back to Poole before answering.

"Might say that there's just a feeling in the air. Some say they can hear it in the wind at night."

"Folks say the moon is blue, you gonna believe it?" Poole grumbled.

Quail's face puzzled. No matter how hard he searched his mind for an answer, there wasn't one that came to mind. He failed to hide his embarrassment.

"I reckon not," Quail deflated.

To his relief, the door suddenly opened, and three upstanding men of the community, joined them. The leader, a man in a well-tailored suit, tipped his hat while eyeing Jones.

"Welcome back, Sheriff."

Jonas Rodgers was about forty and was more perfumed than most lady folk. Deputy Quail coughed a little and tried to hold his nose inconspicuously.

"Thank you, Mayor. Rodgers here is our mayor, and he owns the hotel," Poole announced for Jones' benefit.

Behind Rodgers was barrel-chested Horace Gentry, the same age but not nearly as polished. He was the mayor's right hand for all things indelicate. Next to Gentry stood lanky Clyde Jenkins, a few years younger than the other two. Clyde lacked the look of potential menace that came naturally to Horace, which was why he purposely strummed his skinny fingers against his gun.

Jones nodded at Poole and turned slightly in their direction, letting his hand fall near the gun at his side. If the trio meant to intimidate him, they were sorely disappointed. The grim glare Jones gave them was warning enough.

"So, this is the man we've been waiting to help us," Mayor Rodgers grinned as he reached into his jacket and adjusted his suspenders.

"This here's Jacob Jones," Poole introduced him.

Gentry spat on the floor to his right, just shy of Jones' boots. He flashed a wry smile with a sense of darkness behind it.

"Right proper name for a colored, wouldn't you say, Sheriff?" Gentry inhaled with self-importance. "And one wearing a gun in town? I thought that was against the law."

Jones quickly stepped right up to Gentry and gave him his full attention. Jones stood a good six inches taller than Gentry and made that fact apparent to everyone.

"Man's name's the first thing you ought to get to know before you make any assumptions, mister," Jones said as he stared him down.

"He's here at my behest and afforded all due rights, as any man," Poole replied. "That includes carrying a gun, Gentry."

Jones moved his hand against the wide grip of one of his double-barreled pistols. He undid his notch and continued staring down at Gentry.

"You can call me Mister Jones," he stated.

Gentry swallowed hard. His courage was shaken but not gone as they stood toe-to-toe.

"Fancy gun or no, I don't take that kind of talk from no—"

Rodgers stepped in front of Gentry before he could finish his thought. He gave Jones that kind of smile most smarmy politicians gave. Greasy as his hair oil.

"Ahem. W-what my associate means, Mr. Jones, is we're most appreciative of any help you can provide," Rodgers stammered politely. "I-isn't that right, Mr. Gentry?"

Sheriff Poole quietly put his hand on his gun. Beads of perspiration gathered on Deputy Quail's forehead, as he also brought his hand to his gun.

"*Is* that right, Mr. Gentry?" Jones purposely chided the man.

It was the kind of challenge he knew left Gentry few options, none of them in his favor. Gentry scoffed under his breath before he finally begged off.

"Sheriff Poole made the need clear," Jones replied.

Young Clyde Jenkins noted Jones' weathered uniform. "A Union soldier I see."

"Once on an occasion. Four years," Jones remarked, sticking out his chin.

Clyde nodded approvingly until Gentry elbowed him in the ribs.

"Many a good man lost their lives," Jones measured his words carefully. "White man and colored. All bled the same."

Rodgers nodded in agreement, equally wary of Jones, still unsure what to make of him.

"We're a proud people here in Menifee," Rodgers confessed. "But not too proud to understand that we're dealing with matters beyond our mortal reasoning. I pray you don't judge us too harshly as we wrestle with our fears and imaginings. We are a kind people."

And with that, Mayor Rodgers extended his hand to Jones. A clear mark of Rodger's skill in diplomacy, to which Jones warmly obliged.

"Right neighborly of you," Jones returned.

"Good, then if there is anything you need, Mr. Jones. You'll be kind enough to allow us to oblige." Rodger's gaze quickly fell on Poole. "Within reason, of course."

"Fair enough, Mr. Mayor," Jones nodded.

"Then I expect we shall converse again soon, Mr. Jones. Sheriff," Rodgers tipped his hat again, as he and his men turned to leave.

Poole nodded grimly. Gentry and Jones exchanged one last glare before the men exited.

"Guess Quail was right about there being something in the air," Jones sighed.

Deputy Quail pulled a red rag from his pocket and wiped the sweat with his brow, grateful to have survived the encounter.

"That was a might—"

"—Quail, see your way to getting Mr. Jones settled in," Poole interrupted, "and have Miss Helen send over a good plate for him."

"Yes sir, right away." Quail scurried like a rabbit out the door.

Poole grumbled as he ambled behind his desk. He opened a drawer and grabbed a bottle of whiskey and two glasses. He offered one to Jones.

"Thinking we could both use a taste." Poole filled the glasses.

"These people don't want me here, Sheriff," Jones said, as he picked up his glass.

"These people didn't see what I saw a few weeks ago. They didn't see what you did in Ohio." Poole threw back his shot. "Or whatever was in that barn."

Jones downed his drink and Poole quickly poured him another.

"They need you, Jones. I need you."

It wasn't so much the way he said it, but that Poole said it at all that struck Jones in a way he hadn't considered. Helping a family here and there or some person who encountered a touch of darkness was one thing, but this was something that, according to Poole at least, had already decimated two other towns. For all his sacred gifts had allowed him to do, Jones had yet to encounter the likes of what Poole described.

Just as he raised his glass to toast Poole, they heard it.

A scream.

SEVEN

The sky had turned a tumultuous pale gray as clouds rolled back and forth above the gusty wind. Dust devils sprinted up and down the street as people rushed to see where the sound have come from. The panicked scream drew even Poole, Quail, and Jones into the street. Poole gave Jones a nervous look as they heard more wailing.

"Sounds like it's coming from the livery stable!" Quail pointed.

They barreled down the block and pushed their way through the growing crowd until they reached the center of the commotion. Stocky, unshaven Dennis Hanks was filled with more rage than a man had a right to. His thirty years had worn hard and left him looking like old leather that sat in the sun for far too long. The crowd watched with trepidation as he cursed his daughter, twelve-year-old Virginia. In his shadow, her innocent eyes were filled with stark terror.

"Ungrateful little bitch!" Dennis shouted as he raised a whip high.

"Papa! No! Please!" Virginia pleaded.

Sprawled on the ground behind her was Anna Hanks, Virginia's mother, her garments torn from the sting of the whip in Dennis' hand. Tears, dirt, and blood mixed on her battered face.

"Please, don't hurt Ginny!" Anna pleaded. "Please!"

"Shut up or I'll give ya more!" Dennis shouted at Anna.

She cowered and whimpered. This was not her first beating, but the look on her face said it all. This was nothing like she'd ever experienced before.

Hanks shifted his rage toward Virginia. "I'll teach ya!"

"No! I didn't do it!" Virginia sobbed.

Dennis cracked the whip at the ground beside Virginia. She startled and shrieked as she crept backward toward her mother.

"What the hell is this?" Poole shouted.

The townspeople stared, while Virginia whimpered and tried to inch in the dirt away from her cruel father.

It was indeed the strangest of things. Everyone was transfixed by the moment, as if caught together in some malady of the wind, but Jones knew the truth. Only he had eyes that could see beyond the human veil, beyond the mere confines of mortality. For even as Hanks' neighbors stared at him in unfathomable astonishment, Jones stared at the truth of it. A specter of evil shrouded Hanks. He was possessed by a demon.

Poole began to intercede, but Jones grabbed his arm.

"The hell are you doing?" Poole challenged.

"Maybe you ought to let me take this one, Sheriff," Jones said with a firm hand on Poole's shoulder.

With slight recognition, Poole asked, "This like at the Ketchums?"

Jones nodded silently. Poole righted himself and turned to the crowd.

"Alright now, everybody stay back," Poole instructed. "Let this man handle this."

Poole could feel the weight of every eye fall upon him as the words left his dry lips. The Sheriff of Menifee had just ordered the entire town to follow the lead of a colored man. A stranger who no one had ever laid eyes on before. The impact of it would certainly come back to haunt him in the days to come. Poole glimpsed Parson Greene hovering in the back of the crowd, arms folded. If anyone in town forgot this moment, the minister would be certain to remind them.

"God help us," Poole whispered to Quail.

Quail shuddered. The fear in Poole's eyes reminded the deputy of their visit to Gilly Pines, and he didn't like it one bit. He tried to shake off his confusion at the sheriff giving up authority to Jones.

Suddenly, a woman in a bright blue dress bolted from the crowd, putting herself between the girl and her father. Odessa Grayfoot held the fury of the sun in her dark, almond eyes. She was a child of both Negro and Choctaw blood. Not an uncommon thing, but it was rare that a woman of either ilk would so boldly take a stand. She was defiant in a way not even a white woman would dare.

"You've no cause to hurt this child, Mr. Hanks!" she screamed, as a breeze blew her straight, black hair across her face.

Hanks laughed wickedly and licked his lips. His eyes seemed to roll from side to side in his head. He slid his hand down to his undone pants, making himself a raving spectacle before all.

"You best mind your business," Hanks held his whip out to her threateningly. "Unless you want a taste of what she got coming!"

Odessa glanced back at Virginia and Anna, and the fear in their eyes. She'd seen that fear in many a woman's eye, many a girl barely able to comprehend the toll it demanded on the soul. She turned her gaze back to Hanks and held her ground.

"I won't let you touch her," Odessa spat, seething. "Stay behind me, child."

"Get the hell out of my way, you half-breed bitch!" Hanks fired back.

Odessa's lips trembled as she held up her hunting knife.

"God will see one of us dead first," she replied.

Hanks raised his whip to strike her. "I'll teach ya your place!"

Jones quickly stepped in front of Odessa and raised his hand.

"Menifesini āsiralehu!" he commanded.

Suddenly, Hanks froze, his arm hanging high in the air, unable to move. The whip dangled in the breeze a moment, and then fell from his grip to the dusty ground.

"What the... ?" Quail whispered to Poole, gobsmacked.

"Obey me," Jones ordered.

The wind grew to a howl, and the crowd gasped. Jones stepped forward until he was face-to-face with a drooling and menacing Hanks. Hanks' arm dropped to his side, as if he'd lost control over it.

"W-who the hell are you?" Hanks stammered.

Jones studied him up and down, circling the man. He kicked the whip out of Hanks' range, then reached into his satchel and pulled out a handful of ashes.

"I'll have your name, beast," Jones demanded.

Hanks stared, dumbfounded that Jones would speak to him this way. Fury welled up inside him at the stunned, gawking townspeople behind Jones and Odessa.

"You all hear how this darkie speaks to a white man?" he screamed at the onlookers. "Ain't ya'll gon' do nothin'?"

It all was the proof Poole needed to know this was Jones' element.

"Everybody stay back! This man is working for me!" Poole ordered the crowd.

"Back up, please, ladies," Quail assisted. "Give him some room."

Hanks' face twisted into a grisly, malevolent grimace. Several onlookers gasped when he let out a guttural growl from deep within his throat.

"This body is mine." He looked at Virginia with lust and hatred. "And all that he possesses."

Hanks lunged wildly forward, but Jones easily side-stepped him and threw the ashes in his face. Jones spun the blinded, stumbling Hanks before him and laid his rugged hand atop the man's head.

"You possess nothing!" Jones exclaimed.

With just a touch, all of Dennis Hanks' life, every moment, every feeling he'd ever felt, played out before Jones' eyes. Every joy and every darkness flashed like a montage of moments. A chronicle of his very soul and the grisly evil that wrapped around the heart of this man. An evil that led him to do unspeakable things to himself and his kin, especially the women who loved him. All of it for Jones to bear as an unwilling witness to the shame and depravity that this darkness had not only brought upon Hanks, but that Hanks himself had welcomed it.

Suddenly, a fierce wind whipped up around them, driving the townsfolk backward. A few scattered into nearby buildings, while others fell to their knees and wailed in prayer. Parson Greene and some women ran up the wooden church steps to safety.

Hanks fell to his knees beneath Jones. He frothed at the mouth as Jones chanted above him. Poole fell over Anna to shield her from the gust. Odessa held onto Virginia with all of her strength. Quail gripped a hitching post, frozen to the bone and his mouth agape. The wind sent Mayor Rodgers stumbling from the middle of the street and into Quail's feet. The mayor's hat sailed past them.

"Sweet Mother of God," Rodgers stammered.

Hanks glared up at Jones, spitting vitriol. "I know you, nigga! I see your Black bones!"

"Then see that which will cast you out, demon," Jones proclaimed.

He took the leather cord of black bones from around his neck and held them over Hanks. Hanks let out an ungodly scream. Lightning ripped across the sky and thunder shook the ground beneath them. Panicked townspeople ran in all directions as the wind howled. The bones in Jones' hand rattled over Hanks, who twisted and turned as if being beaten about under the power of this enchantment.

"Tell me your name!!" Jones screamed, watching the evil shroud move around Hanks.

"I'll see this body torn apart!" Hanks responded in a demonic tone for all to hear.

Jones narrowed his eyes on Hanks and chanted. "Menifesini āsiralehu!"

Hanks rose from his knees and stood. His eyes grew vacant.

"Ganēni simihini nigerenyi!" Jones shouted in his native tongue.

Hanks' feet slowly lifted from the ground and his eyes rolled back.

"By the spirits!" Odessa exclaimed, as little Virginia shrieked beneath her.

Black Bones Jones' eyes turned full black.

"Ganēni simihini!" he chanted over and over. "Ganēni simihini!"

A bolt of lightning flashed and struck Jones and Hanks, sending them crumbling to the ground. They lay there smoldering.

"Sweet Lord in Heaven," Poole prayed, still holding onto Anna.

Everything and everyone were silent and still, until Odessa rushed up beside Jones' body. She rolled him onto his back and placed her hands on his charred chest to feel for movement. She put her head on his heart. No breath and no heartbeat. She began to chant in her native tongue.

Suddenly, Jones sucked in a loud, gasping breath. Quail and the mayor, still hanging onto each other, gasped in awe. Poole rose to his feet, slowly. Townspeople cautiously emerged from their scattered places, murmuring at the supernatural scene before them.

Odessa sat upright. "You'll be fine, stranger."

As Jones' breathing returned to normal, he rolled up onto his knees. He locked eyes on Odessa with an unusual intensity. His gaze lingered on her hair as it floated on the dying breeze. There was a hint of a smile on the corner of her lips.

"It's Jones," he replied. "Thank you. Miss…"

"Odessa. Odessa Grayfoot." She pulled out a handkerchief and dabbed at his face.

"Mighty thankful for your kindness."

Odessa leaned close to his ear and whispered, "Be careful who you trust in this town, Jones."

Before he could respond, she stood up and spun back toward the center of town, disappearing into the reconvening crowd. Gone like the wind itself. Bewildered, Jones pushed up to his feet. He slung his satchel over his shoulder and slipped the necklace of bones back around his neck. Poole helped Anna to her feet, then stepped up next to Jones.

"Jones?"

"No worse for wear," Jones replied. "I'm alright, Sheriff."

Poole nodded and patted Jones' shoulder, then went to check on Virginia and Anna. Hanks moaned, finally stirring. Jones glared at him, then started to brush the dirt from his hands. He paused, astonished. His fingers were covered in blood. His gifts had always protected him from harm. He'd only ever been injured once. The facial scar he got the night he defended his mother as the Jones plantation burned to the ground.

"Momma!" Virginia called out as she sprinted into her mother's arms.

Jones watched them embrace, remembering and missing his own mother. He looked down at his hands again, but this time, there was no blood.

"The hell'd ya do to me?" Hanks lumbered to his feet, still groggy from the encounter.

"Just helped you is all," Jones remarked.

Hanks gazed back at his family, who recoiled with dread.

"Why's the Sheriff with my wife?" Hanks turned to Jones. "What did ya do to my woman?"

"You best tend to them," Jones exhaled.

Jones dusted himself off and winced as he hobbled away. But Hanks was far from satisfied with Jones' answer. He bolted to his feet and chased Jones to grab him and spin him around.

"Boy, I should kill ya where ya stand! I'll see ya hanged!" Hanks threatened.

Without a word, Jones grabbed Hanks by the throat and squeezed tight. Townsfolk gasped and gawked. Feeling their eyes on him, Jones loosened his grip, then grabbed the front of Hanks' shirt.

"Maybe they should hang you for what you've been thinking about that little girl," Jones pulled him close. "Maybe I ought to tell them how you opened yourself to that demon inside you."

Hanks paled as he felt Jones' hot breath sting his face. "I ain't done nothing wrong," he choked out his words.

"I know your soul, Hanks," Jones raged. "I saw what you've done and to whom." Jones' gaze fell back to Anna. "Your own wife's sister."

"How — how could you know that?" Hanks trembled.

"You've damned your own soul," Jones explained. "Best thing you could do for your family is leave town forever."

Jones shoved him to the ground. Hanks shrank before him.

"Or maybe I'll just tell the Sheriff," Jones threatened.

Hanks swallowed hard as he stared into the eyes of the townsfolk, looking at him with utter disdain. They saw him as he truly was for the very first time, and they did not approve.

"Y'all take the word of a colored over mine? It wasn't me, ya hear! It wasn't me!"

But Hanks' pleas fell on deaf ears. No one raised a voice in support. Beaten and disgraced, he scrambled for the stable.

Jones scanned the scene, not sure if he'd made the townsfolk more fearful of him or faithful to see how he could help them. But those thoughts would have to wait as the sound of a charging horse drew him. He turned to see Hanks riding hard atop a horse.

"You'll curse the day!" Hanks cried out. "I swear ya all will!"

Poole pulled Anna and Virginia out of the way just as Hanks charged past them. Jones sidestepped Hanks and his horse as they rode out of town. The howling wind followed him until they both disappeared in the fading light.

Poole kicked up some dust as he made his way over to Jones. "Was that the—?"

Jones shook his head before Poole could finish his question.

"—Shroud demon. Strong sum bitch."

"How you mean?" Poole asked.

Jones inched closer to Poole, away from prying ears. "Dark things like that need an invitation. You invite it in you. The longer it stays, the stronger it gets. Been feeding off that one for a long time. But it ain't what I'm here for."

"Shit. Fuck." Poole cursed under his breath.

"In more ways than you can imagine, Sheriff."

"How so? I mean, are we—"

"—There's more darkness here than you could imagine," Jones explained. "This ain't like a bee in your bonnet. This is more like a hornet's nest that's been living behind the walls."

Poole didn't miss the fact that Jones wouldn't look him in the eye and kept his head hung low. Jones stared at the scorched earth where the lightning struck, but the dirt wasn't black. It was a deep, dark red.

"And it's everywhere, Sheriff," Jones said. "It's everywhere."

EIGHT

Poole couldn't tear himself away from the foreboding look on Jones' face, nor the sinking feeling that sat in the pit of his stomach like a lead stone. He shook his head at Parson Greene, who now lurked on the periphery of the gathering townsfolk, close enough to eavesdrop. Poole reached into his pocket and pulled out his handkerchief.

"Does it always do that to ya?" he lowered his voice, as held his handkerchief out to Jones.

"Ain't always the same." Jones held the cloth to his mouth. "But then all evil ain't the same either."

"How's that so?" Poole asked.

Before Jones could answer, Mayor Rodgers bounded in front of them. His face was full of excitement, like a child who just caught their first firefly. Poole rolled his eyes at the envy on the parson's face as Rodgers extended his hand to Jones.

"Mister Jones, I must apologize for any skepticism of you on my part."

"He's everything we heard he was," Poole chimed in.

Rodgers gave Poole a dismissive glance. "Indeed. The kind of man Menifee needs."

Poole smiled to himself when Parson Greene kicked the dirt and huffed off toward the church.

Unimpressed by the mayor's flattery, Jones replied, "If it's all the same to you, I need to clear the dust outta my throat."

Rodgers abruptly grabbed Jones by the arm, leading him off with Poole in tow.

"I'm sure we can get you all fixed up," Rodgers assured. "My slave quarters are some of the best in the county. You won't be disappointed."

Jones stopped cold in his tracks. His jaw clenched. Rodgers turned to meet his glare.

"You own slaves?" Jones' question came with razor-sharp bite.

Rodgers glanced at Poole. "Well, that is to say—"

"—My recollection serves right," Jones cut him off, "I fought and killed men so no one would be called slave ever again."

Rodgers swallowed hard, clearly not expecting Jones' reaction.

"Now see here, Jones. I'm not accustomed to being told what I can or cannot do with my property."

Jones squared his shoulders and stood face-to-face with Rodgers. The rage in his eyes was clear, but he knew how to temper his words until he had cause not to.

"I stand corrected. I thought they were people, not livestock," Jones snapped.

Jones turned his gaze back to Poole, who stood speechless. Poole was at a loss for a way to engage in the struggle before him. For the second time in a day, he felt utterly powerless. It was yet another situation he'd never thought he'd be in, let alone in front of the growing crowd of curious townsfolk.

Rodgers adjusted his coat. "I don't see any problem."

"No problem at all, sir," Jones glared at Poole. "Best have Quail bring my wagon back. I'll be taking my leave."

Without another word, Jones started toward the Sheriff's office, leaving both men dismayed and dumbfounded. Would he actually leave, just like that?

"Jones, wait," Poole followed him. "We had a deal!"

Rodgers hurried to keep up with them.

"Funny how you left out the part about these people owning slaves," Jones remarked.

"Dammit, Jones! How could I have told you?" Poole pleaded.

"You had a choice." Jones hissed. "War's been over, and you act like it didn't happen."

Poole sprinted ahead of Jones to backpedal in front of him.

"You know what we're up against, Jones. How can you walk away?"

This time Jones doesn't temper his words. "You really expect me to do for yours while you still—I'm done."

In an act of desperation, Poole drew his gun. His hand shook as he took aim at Jones.

"Don't make me shoot you," Poole struggled to put courage behind his claim.

Jones stared at him coldly. "Be good enough to shoot me while I'm looking at you."

Neither man uttered a word as they stood there in the dying light of day. This was the last place either of them wanted to be, and far too often this was the inevitable scene between white man and colored. But today would not end as so many others had. Poole lowered his gun, his eyes damp as he made one desperate last plea.

"Back on the trail, I could have let those slavers take you," he reminded Jones. "But I did right by you, Jones. All I'm asking is that you keep your word to me. Please."

Jones sighed and chewed on it for a moment. Then he tossed his gaze back at Rodgers.

"I gave you my word I'd help, Sheriff," Jones admitted. "Since Mayor Rodgers said I could have anything I need, I'll start with some new clothes, and a saddle for my horse. And I'll see every slave freed, to help this town."

"I-I said anything within reason," Rodgers stammered.

Jones walked up to Rodgers. "Seems reasonable to me, seeing that slavery ain't something we no longer allow in this land. A few slaves for the soul of this town." Jones turned to Poole. "Seem fair to you, Sheriff?"

Poole heaved a heavy sigh. He met Rodgers' icy grimace. Poole was many things, but he'd always been a man of his word.

"Damn fair, Mr. Jones," Poole answered.

"Now see here!" Rodgers shouted.

Poole moved in closer, so close Rodgers could feel his stinging breath on him.

"You willing to lose everything over your pride, Rodgers?" Poole demanded. "The man's right and you damn well know it! It's been law for three years, and the war's over for months now."

Rodgers felt angry and humiliated. He instinctively reached for his gun. The crowd that followed behind them murmured, expecting another confrontation. But Rodgers was a savvy politician, and he knew that acting in the heat of the moment could wreak havoc on his career, not to mention his hotel business.

"Common sense says saving the town is what we all want." Rodgers forced a smile and held his hand out to Jones. "I agree to your terms, Mr. Jones."

Jones took his hand with a grin. "Mighty neighborly of you, Mayor."

Rodgers wasted no time in using the moment to curry the town's favor. He turned to the crowd. "Good people, Mr. Jones has agreed to save us from our troubles! Let us welcome him as a friend and neighbor!" he announced.

Rodgers waded back into the warm embrace of the people of Menifee, satisfied that he had again done right by them. A few of the townsfolk kept suspicious eyes on Poole and Jones, awash with loathing and fear, and not just against the dark-skinned man in their midst. But most of the crowd rallied around Rodgers and followed him back to the center of town.

Jones turned to Poole. "No more secrets, Sheriff."

"My word on it, no question," Poole replied.

Jones noticed a lone figure with an eerie countenance staring at him. Willa Stanton's face brightened with a wide smile as she bounced and clapped her hands.

"I told you," she cried out. "I told you he was the one!"

Jones and Poole paled as she turned with a lilt in her step and danced away down the street. Whatever inspired this confidence Willa had in Jones—a belief that no one would take away from her—only time would reveal the weight of it. Only time would prove the evidence of her faith.

"Jones," Poole inquired, "what did you mean before when you said there's more darkness than I can imagine? What do you see that I can't?"

Jones opened his mouth to speak, but felt an icy chill run over the back of his neck. He pivoted sharply, as if someone or something touched him. But this peculiar touch wasn't strange or out of the ordinary. In fact, this was familiar, like the touch of your mother's hand as it caressed your cheek. He wondered if there was something about this town that knew him, but how? He'd never set foot in Menifee before today.

"Jones?"

"Maybe we just leave it be for a spell, Sheriff." Jones peered up and down the street.

Poole watched silently as Jones walked away.

***

Menifee only had one saloon, but it was one of the finer places in town. The floors were clean and well-constructed, and despite the occasional dust-up among folks who had too much to drink, it had a neighborly quality to it.

It had been hours since the melee at the livery stable. The folks who hadn't gone home to pray found themselves washing the day away with a different kind of spirit. Among them was Sheriff Poole, who purposely sat alone at the end of the bar, with no desire for company nor any comfort he couldn't find in the bottom of a glass. He nursed the last remnants from a bottle of whiskey. He was bold-faced drunk and didn't give a damn who saw him. And after all that he'd seen in the last few days, no one could rightly blame him.

Poole had been the kind of man who only knew ordinary evil, such that would steal a horse or shoot a man in the back. But from the day he met Jones, he'd witnessed extraordinary evil that most folks tell their young ones about to keep them on the straight and narrow. And until now, Poole never really believed in any evil that a jail couldn't contain. But all of that changed when he met Jones.

At a table behind him, huddled over their own bottle, sat Rodgers, Jenkins, and Gentry. They grumbled over the implications that came with Jones since his arrival in Menifee.

"Just ain't right, boss," Gentry bemoaned.

"You saw what he did out there, practically summoned the whirlwind," Jenkins exclaimed.

"Wouldn't have believed it if I hadn't seen it with my own eyes," Rodgers downed a shot of whiskey and poured another. "He's not at all like the other Negroes."

"But freeing all your slaves?" Gentry asked aloud.

Rodgers cut his eyes to Gentry, then Jenkins, staring them down. "You mind your tongues. I'm simply biding my time until this crisis has passed."

"God willing we all live that long," Poole called out from the bar.

Rodgers gave Poole an incredulous glare. "Might, if you tried harder to find a white man to solve our problems."

Poole spun off his stool and faced them.

"It always comes back to that for you, don't it?" Poole gritted. "The man saved a child, but that's not enough for ya, is it?"

"I give credit where it's due, Sheriff," Rodgers fired back. "But the cost is another matter altogether."

"Is that how you value life? Is that how you see another man's worth?" Poole returned.

Rodgers rubbed the rim of his glass. "By my account, I've given more than my share in flesh and blood for Menifee. A father, mother, two brothers to the war, and even a young wife who died in childbirth."

"We've all lost someone, Mayor," Poole grunted. "Your suffering ain't no greater than any man or woman here."

Rodgers rose from his seat. He marched up to Poole with his fists clenched and an arrogant sneer on his face.

"Perhaps, Sheriff. But I have never bent the knee to a nigger," Rodgers remarked.

Poole's eyes filled with fury as he fought to stay seated on the stool. He tightly gripped the empty bottle.

"Can you say the same?" Rodgers' question cut deep.

A hush fell over the saloon as all eyes watched them. Rodgers' eyes bulged as he worked to keep his rage in check for their audience. Poole thought about how easily he could crush Rodgers' throat, and the bottle in his hand cracked. Despite the overwhelming urge to give Rodgers the beating of his life, he knew that there were certain expectations that came with his job as sheriff. And being a bully wasn't on the list.

"Ain't you got slaves to set free, Mr. Mayor?" Poole sneered back.

He stood erect, startling Rodgers by his sudden move. Poole was a half foot taller than Rodgers, and glared down at him until he blinked. He sighed with a heavy rattle in his chest, noting Rodgers' men leering at him. Without a word, Poole turned to the door and left.

After stumbling from the saloon in a huff, and with a bladder beyond full, Poole found himself in an alley. With much procession at his waist, he relieved himself on the side of the saloon. With a great sigh of relief, he shook his head to rid the whiskey-induced throbbing in his temples. The sting of Rodgers' words still hung like a dark cloud over him. Poole was a man caught in the dichotomy of doing what he believed was best for his town and the beliefs many folks still held about being a white man. A social norm for some, a stigma to others. But Rodgers questioned more than

Poole's racial identity. He cast doubt on his integrity, and that was something Poole couldn't stomach.

Suddenly, he heard the soft patter of footsteps behind him. He quickly finished redressing and turned to see a Choctaw child. Her long dark hair was in ponytails that hung to her wrists. She shook a rattlesnake's tail in front of her. Poole could hear her softly singing in her native tongue, but the tune was familiar—*Amazing Grace*.

"Hey, what're you doing out here?" Poole slurred.

She stopped long enough to acknowledge Poole with her coal-black eyes. She shook her rattle at him, then ran away giggling.

"Hey!" Poole called out.

Poole stumbled out of the alley and onto the street, chasing the girl who seemed to stay just beyond his reach. He struggled to keep his feet beneath him as the child's pace quickened. Even in his drunken state, Poole tried his best to close the gap, but each time he reached her, she swiftly darted in a different direction. She led him to the edge of town before she finally vanished into the shadows between the last two buildings. Only the sound of her rattle lingered in the dark. Poole stopped at the buildings and held onto his knees, out of breath.

"Kid, where'd ya go?" Poole panted.

Poole shuffled into the shadows, feeling his way as he moved further into the darkness.

"Hello? Kid? Where are you?"

A giggle echoed as though it were a hundred miles away. Poole reached out and saw his hand disappear into the shadows before him. A coldness ran up through his arm and into his chest, forcing him to gasp for air. He was of a mind to draw back, but something grabbed his arm. It held him with unbelievable strength. Poole jerked back hard to no avail. He was frozen where he stood, caught by whatever had him.

"The hell?" Poole tried to pull away. "Let go of me, dammit!"

From the darkness, another giggle, but much darker than the last. Sinister. He felt the blood drain from his face, suddenly sober as fear coursed through him.

"Who's there?"

There was nothing. No sound, save for his shallow breath. He heard an angry growl, low and bestial, coming closer from inside the darkness. Poole leaned back for all he was worth, desperate to free himself. Something yanked him into the shadows. His muffled screams sounded like he was a thousand miles away.

A final giggle filled the night, then the steady beat of distant drums grew louder and louder and then — silence.

NINE

Morning came early for Deputy Quail. He leisurely made his rounds, checking doors and making sure some drunkard from the night before hadn't drowned in the horse troughs. He whistled his way from one building to another, eventually making his way to the Sheriff's office.

Quail struggled a moment to adjust his gun belt, then marched up the steps. He was surprised to find the door open.

"Sheriff?" Quail quizzically peered in.

He stepped in and looked around. "Sheriff?"

He scurried from one side of the office to the other, checking behind the desk. No Sheriff.

"Sheriff Poole?"

With a shrug, he shut the front door behind him. Quail grabbed an apple from the desk and headed to the jail cells at the back of the building. He polished the apple on his shirt, then opened his mouth to take a big bite, but halted. The door to the last cell was wide open, swaying back and forth.

"Hello? Anybody here?" Quail called out.

He slid next to the opposite wall and inched closer to the cell. A scratching noise made him full stop again. He drew his gun.

"Sheriff Poole?" he called out again.

With an apple in one hand and his gun shaking in the other, Quail mustered as much courage as he could find and slowly peeked into the open cell. What he found nearly made him drop everything. He stared in shock and disbelief.

It was Sheriff Poole, though in a state far from anything Quail could have ever imagined. Poole was crouched in the cell over a small fire, with a white streak painted across his weathered face. He'd stripped down to nothing more than a torn piece of cloth covering his groin.

"Jesus, Sh-Sheriff," Quail stammered.

Poole chanted indistinctly and gestured over the fire, rocking back and forth in a childlike cadence. He looked up at Quail with a mouth full of blood.

"Sweet Lord!" Quail exclaimed.

Quail bolted from the Sheriff's office, running as fast as his feet would carry him down the street.

"Mr. Jones! Mr. Jones!" the deputy screamed.

He darted into the livery and made a beeline for Jones' wagon. He leapt up into the back, only to find it empty.

"Mr. Jones! I need help!" Quail shouted.

Just then Jones emerged from the stalls, tying off his trousers and wiping sleep from his eyes.

"Quail? The hell you going on about?"

Quail grabbed him by the arm. "It's the Sheriff, something's happened to him!"

"Hold on, what do you mean?" Jones asked.

Quail took a deep breath and tried to gather his thoughts.

"The Sheriff," Quail said between gasps. "He's acting like a man possessed."

Jones didn't waste time asking questions. He grabbed his gun belt and satchel from the wagon and turned back to Quail.

"Take me to him," Jones said.

***

As they arrived at the Sheriff's office, Quail paused in the street. The trepidation on the young man's face told Jones everything he needed to know.

"It's okay, Quail," Jones said softly. "I got this."

Quail nodded, thankful, as his lips trembled. "I'll go get Doc Willis."

Quail ran for help, like he'd been shot out of a cannon. In a way, Jones felt sorry for him. This would leave the kind of mark on Quail's soul that he'd never truly understand, but would forever haunt him. It was as though he were watching the young man's innocence being ripped away forever. That was something he wouldn't wish on no man.

Once inside, Jones padded carefully through the office, back to the jail cells. As he approached the last cell, the skin on the back of his neck prickled.

"Poole?" he called out.

Jones halted at the sight of Poole, who bit down hard into a dead rabbit, tearing its flesh away clear to the bone. His eyes cut to Jones as he ripped off a hunk and swallowed it whole.

"Damn," Jones braced himself.

Poole watched curiously as Jones took a handful of ash and sprinkled it across the doorway. Like some kind of animal, he sniffed at Jones before he growled, low and guttural.

"Easy, Poole. Nice and easy," Jones said as he knelt down to spread a second line of ash across the floor. He chanted softly. Poole glared, crouching low and ready to pounce.

With a small piece of charcoal from his satchel, Jones scribbled between the two lines, drawing letters and shapes from one end to the other until he'd completed his enchantment. As he stood again, his eyes met Poole's beast-like gaze. Gone was the man he'd only known for a short time, replaced by something Jones could barely comprehend.

"What the hell happened to you?" Jones asked aloud.

"Is he okay, Mr. Jones?" Quail called from down the hall.

Instinctively, Jones turned to the sound of Quail's voice, and for a fraction of a second, he took his eyes off Poole. It was all the time Poole needed. He lunged at Jones, teeth bared, careening for his throat. Mid-air, Poole slammed against the invisible protective barrier Jones had set. He fell back to the floor, screaming. Indeed, he would have succeeded had the enchantment not held him at bay.

"Mr. Jones? Is h-he okay?" Quail called again.

"Not quite," Jones answered Quail.

Poole struggled, writhing on the floor. Jones knelt again and laid his hand on Poole's head.

"*Menifesini āsiralehu*," Jones chanted in his native tongue.

Poole's eyes turned white, and suddenly the whole of Poole's life flashed before Jones's eyes. Every day Poole had lived fluttered by like leaves caught in a great wind until settling on the haunting image of the Choctaw child. But then, something strange happened. The child turned from Poole to look right at Jones. She could see him.

The child's eyes grew dark and foreboding and in that same moment, something else happened to Poole. His eyes were no longer white, but feral once more. Somehow, the enchantment had been broken and Poole lunged again, overpowering Jones, who fell back against the floor.

"Shit," Jones cursed.

He used his arm to keep Poole at bay. Quail rushed in and tried to help, but Poole shoved him back with an unnatural ferocity. Quail tumbled into the adjacent cell.

"*Menifesini āsiralehu!!*" Jones shouted, but nothing happened.

He chanted again, louder and louder, but Poole kept up his attack, somehow growing stronger with each attempt. With his free hand, Jones punched him in the face over and over until Poole staggered, but he was far from beaten. Jones scrambled to his feet seconds before Poole charged again. This time, Jones unrelentingly smashed his fist into Poole, striking one brutal blow after another until Poole finally fell.

"Fuck me," Jones dropped back against the wall, sucking wind.

Having regained himself, Quail rushed to Jones' side.

"Mr. Jones," Quail stammered. "Are you hurt?"

"Ain't dead," Jones gasped. "I reckon I'm all right."

Quail held out his hand and helped Jones to his feet.

"Ain't never seen nothing like that before," Quail exclaimed. "Did ya beat the demon outta him, Mr. Jones?"

They turned to Poole, only to gaze upon a much different man than they faced moments ago. Poole had curled himself into a ball and wept like a baby on the floor beneath them.

"Sweet Lord," Quail gasped.

***

Menifee was fortunate to have an experienced doctor who had kept many of the gravely ill from a dark fate and attended the births of more than half the town's children. Doc Willis had the kindest eyes in all of Menifee, a feature that served him well.

Jones and Quail carried Poole to the good doctor's door, somehow avoiding prying eyes and dubious glances. Doc Willis' modest office was not much different from any of the other buildings in town, save for the jars filled with medical instruments and bottles of liniment and bandages. They laid Poole upon the doctor's table. Willis stood over Poole and examined him from head to toe.

Jones leaned against the doorway, intently watching the doctor. Quail paced back and forth, nervous and bewildered. Poole writhed and twisted, beset by something unseen. Willis turned to Jones with a doleful look in his eyes.

"Not sure what to make of it." Doc Willis scratched his head.

"What's wrong with his face?" Quail inquired.

"That's not paint, it's in his skin," Willis explained. "He's wound up tight as a rattler."

"When I first saw him, he kept mumbling something about the ground," Quail stated.

Jones pivoted toward Quail. "What about the ground?"

Quail wiped his brow with a trembling hand. "Ain't rightly sure, but something about the blood on the ground."

"You didn't think to mention that when you came after me?" Jones glared.

Quail shifted nervously, "I was—well... I-I was worried about the Sheriff."

There was no sense in arguing about it. Jones knew Quail was barely hanging on by a thread at the sight of Poole in such a state. But what troubled him more was how Poole had broken the enchantment. Had he not laid the ash properly? Perhaps Jones stepped in the ash and broke it accidentally without realizing it. Whatever the reason, Jones knew he'd come inches from losing his own life, though God help him, he didn't understand why.

"Normally I'd say it was the fever, but he doesn't have none." Willis shrugged. Poole groaned, then rolled to one side and vomited on the floor.

"Easy, Sheriff," Willis turned back to him, but Poole pushed him away.

"Jones... Jones." Poole strained between gasps. Jones stepped up to the table and bent down over Poole.

"I'm here," Jones answered. "What happened to you, Sheriff?"

Poole looked up at him with glazed eyes and tried to smile. Then he writhed in agony, seized by a sudden pain that made him convulse wildly. He grabbed Jones' hand and held on tight until the pain relented.

"Tell me how to help you," Jones urged.

But try as he might, Poole couldn't make the words come, at least not in a way that made sense to any of them. He swallowed hard and tried to focus with all his might on Jones.

"Up... to you now," Poole stammered, before another stab of pain sent him reeling. "Gave... me... your word."

Jones laid a hand on his shoulder. "I gave you my word, Sheriff. I intend to keep it."

Through tears, Poole nodded and brought his hand up to his chest. Jones tracked his hand as Poole reached for his badge.

"Take it," Poole gritted.

Confused, Jones held his hand over Poole's. Poole opened his palm and placed his badge in Jones' hand. Both Quail and Doc Willis stood there in shock.

"The blood, Jones." Poole strained as his eyes fell on Quail. "Save my town."

Overcome with pain, Poole arched his back high, then lost consciousness. His hand fell away, leaving Jones with his badge. Jones stood tall and stared at Willis and Quail in disbelief.

"Reckon that means you're the Sheriff now, Mister," Willis said.

"Ain't I supposed to swear on a bible or something?" Jones asked.

Doc Willis reached into his desk and pulled out an old bible. He held it out in front of Jones.

"You swear not to kill nobody that don't try to kill you first?" Willis asked.

Jones placed his hand on the bible, "Reckon I do."

"Congratulations, you're the Sheriff." Willis proclaimed.

"Sweet Lord, help us," Quail shook his head.

"Amen to that, Quail," Jones agreed. "Amen to that."

Moments later, Jones strode into the street with Quail in tow. He stared down at the badge in his hand as the weight of it hit him like an iron slug to the chest. Saving a town was one thing, he had done that before, but convincing these folks he was their new sheriff was uncharted territory, even for him. Quail strode next to him.

"Ain't never had no colored Sheriff in Menifee before," Quail stated.

"I reckon you haven't."

"I did hear tell of a colored U.S. Marshall. Is he kin to you?" Quail asked.

"You think all colored men is kin, Quail?" Jones fired back.

"Well, y'all all came from the same place, didn't ya?"

Jones glared, ignoring Quail's question. "Get a pair of fresh horses and supplies for the night. We're going for a ride."

"Where to?" Quail inquired.

Jones sighed, remembering his promise to Poole. He put the badge on.

"Gilly Pines," Jones replied, as he reached the sheriff's office.

Quail's feet halted. With a trembling hand, he pulled his handkerchief from his pocket and wiped his face, now pale at the haunting memory of Gilly Pines.

***

Jones sat brooding in Poole's chair, his mind racing about the events that had transpired and how he was going to keep his promise. He got up and poured himself a cup of coffee when Mayor Rodgers and Parson Greene suddenly burst in.

"Sheriff Poole," Rodgers stopped in his tracks at the sight of Jones. "Where's the Sheriff?"

Jones considered for a moment and then turned to Rodgers and Greene. The look on their faces was all that Jones expected and more. Rodgers stared with his jaw hung low, not so much at Jones as he did the badge on his chest. Greene crossed his arms.

"What's the meaning of this?" Rodgers stammered.

"Why are you wearing that?" the parson demanded.

"Sheriff Poole has taken ill," Jones replied. "He asked me to fill in for him."

"Impossible." Rodgers stammered.

"Yet here I am," Jones sipped his coffee. "Doc Willis and Deputy Quail witnessed it."

Parson Greene swallowed hard, not sure how to digest this. The mayor and the minister exchanged looks of concern. Rodgers tugged at his jacket, trying to compose himself. Greene finally found his voice.

"I don't know if this is the Lord's will," he asserted.

Jones frowned, but kept his eyes on his coffee. No need to acknowledge Greene's jealousy.

"And I'm not sure the townsfolk will be agreeable to this," the mayor surmised.

"Reckon most won't, but it ain't them I made a promise to," Jones took another sip.

Rodgers studied him carefully. Jones had already gained favor with his exploits in the Hanks situation, and this would put the mayor at odds with him yet again. He had to be calculated in this.

"Parson, perhaps I could have a moment to discuss government business with our new sheriff?"

Parson Greene, at a loss for words, left in a huff. Rodgers closed the door behind him, then turned to Jones.

"Suppose this is all true. To what end does it serve?" he inquired.

"Sheriff Poole wasn't the kind of man to mince words. Whatever he feared was coming to this town, he believed I could stop it. I intend to keep my word."

"And can you?" Rodgers needled further. "Can you stop it?"

Jones studied Rodgers now. He tried to discern the man from the politician, neither of whom he truly trusted. He set the cup of coffee on Poole's desk.

"First thing I need is answers," Jones replied. "Poole said he'd seen the aftermath of whatever he thinks is coming this way. If'n there's a way for me to know what he saw—"

"—You'd know how to stop it," Rodgers interjected.

Jones nodded. "Seeing as how we all benefit from me making this happen expeditiously, I'd hope to have you support me in my brief time as a lawman here."

Rodgers raised an eyebrow, realizing there was a play for him in all of this that could still work in his favor. He smiled brightly at Jones and reached for the door.

"For the sake of the town, of course. I'll make it plain to the townsfolk you'll be acting sheriff until Poole returns. Rest assured, you have my full support. And don't worry about the minister. He'll see things my way."

"Much obliged, Mr. Mayor," Jones responded as Rodgers opened the door. "And I'll make sure the Sheriff knows you had no issue bending the knee as it were."

Rodger froze, the color running from his face. He turned slowly back to Jones, who glared at him darkly over the rim of his coffee cup. How did Jones know what he'd said to Poole? Jones gave him a nod. Rodgers bolted from the office.

Through the front window, Jones watched Rodgers and Greene storm off as another pair appeared, headed in his direction. Quail trotted down the street on horseback as Odessa kept pace next to him. Jones donned his hat as the two entered the sheriff's office.

"Miss Odessa," Jones acknowledged her.

"Quail tells me you plan on heading to Gilly Pines," Odessa announced.

Jones glared at Quail. "Did he now?"

"You'd be wise to take me with you," she asserted.

"Why's that?" Jones folded his arms over his chest.

"I know these trails better than anyone," Odessa explained. "You're already half the morning gone and won't be back before dark. God knows you'll be lost before you realize it."

Jones finished his coffee and sighed. From the look Quail tried to hide, she was indeed right about everything she said, and time was not his ally at the moment.

"I guess I'd be most appreciative of that kind of experience," Jones admitted.

Odessa grabbed a rifle from the wall and grinned at him. "Damn right, you would."

He smiled to himself, following Quail and Odessa through the door.

As he mounted his horse, Jones felt the eyes of the townsfolk staring in his direction, not simply at the man, but the fact he'd replaced Poole as sheriff. No one raised their voice in discontent, but you could see it in their eyes. At best, folks didn't rightly know what to make of it. A few faces held disdain, disgust, and even rage at the very thought of Jones as sheriff. Clearly, not a man or woman among them was pleased at this turn of events.

In front of the hotel, the mayor and the minister waved at them with tight smiles, obviously hoping Jones would fail.

Odessa turned her horse in front of Jones, smiling as she blocked his view.

"Best we be moving on, Sheriff," she urged.

She kicked her horse and started off. Quail gave him a sympathetic look and followed her.

"I got a bad feeling," Jones muttered, setting off after them.

TEN

An hour later, they were deep into their arduous ride, covering miles as they chased the sun. Quail lagged a few paces behind Jones and Odessa, still not as comfortable in the saddle as most men his age. Jones paid close attention to Odessa. He admired how well she handled her horse, skilled and confident, with a kind of regal air about her. There was something he found quite appealing in the way she held her head high, embracing the wind across her face.

Odessa glanced in his direction and tracked the look on his face for a moment before she spoke.

"Not used to seeing a woman ride the way a man does?"

"Can't say I've known many who do," Jones replied. "Get out riding much, do you?"

Odessa gently stroked her horse's mane as her hair fell over her face.

"I grew up with this horse," she smiled. "We've been together all our lives. We are like family to each other."

"Guess it comes with the job."

"You mean leading my people?" Odessa inquired. "Colored ain't never have a woman lead them before?"

"That ain't what I'm saying." Jones corrected.

"Then what are you saying, Jones?" Odessa chided him.

He chewed on it, but he had nothing.

"I'm saying I need to work on keeping my foot outta my mouth." He adjusted his hat.

She chuckled. He smiled. It was a light moment they shared in a time when such things were rare, if not altogether non-existent, especially for people like them.

"Guess it comes with the job." Odessa grinned.

"You ain't gon' let that pass, are ya?"

Odessa shook her head. "Knowing how fond you are of the taste of your foot? What do you think?"

"Just making sure is all," he replied.

They both laughed aloud as Quail finally caught up to them.

"I miss something?" Quail puzzled.

The confused look on his face somehow made it funnier, and Jones and Odessa burst into laughter.

***

It was near dusk by the time they arrived at Gilly Pines, and the stench of death was more repellant than before. The horses bristled nervously as they crossed the outskirts where the smell of burned flesh still hung heavy in the air. They all tied on bandanas before riding into town, and not just to mask the smell. Even burned death brought disease that they couldn't risk taking back to Menifee.

Piles of ash had collected like small dunes, blown by the wind. They resembled pillars to the carnage. As they made their way down the main street, it was clear that the darkness that had fallen over this town left nothing and no one unscathed. Jones noticed Quail was more skittish than his horse.

"Deputy?" Jones called out.

Quail startled and turned toward Jones. "Yes sir?"

"Might be best if you guard the perimeter a ways back," Jones suggested. "Keep me and Miss Odessa safe while we ride through."

Quail gave him a thankful nod. "Yes sir!"

Quail turned tail swiftly and rode back to the edge of town.

"Don't judge him too harshly," Odessa said. "He's a little more than a child."

"I've kinda taken a shine to him," Jones told her. "No need for his soul to become as dark as mine has."

Odessa felt the pain in his words. She discovered a vulnerable tenderness in him that surprised her. But she knew that sound in a man's voice. A man who'd seen far more darkness than anyone should, and without seeing it, she knew it had left a scar on the soul of Black Bones Jones.

He dismounted and handed his reins to Odessa. An intuitive impulse urged her to caution him.

"Be careful, Jones."

His eyes met hers for a moment. The wind shifted her hair so that it cascaded around her face, framing her beauty and her fierceness against the golden pink sunset. She was a portrait that would be forever etched in his mind, and he considered himself lucky to have seen her. He tried to speak, but the words suddenly got caught in his throat. All he could do was offer a polite nod before he turned toward the town on foot.

Gilly Pines had become hell on earth, or at least as close as any man should come to see it. As Jones stepped past the incinerated hunks of the remains of the town's people, a chill came over him. It reminded him of that fateful boyhood night when he and his kin watched the Jones plantation burn to the ground. He could still hear the screams with each body he passed. With every mound of seared flesh, a memory of the night and the Inky Thing that took his mother, changing his life in ways that no one could have possibly imagined. Instinctively, his hand went to the lightning scar on his face.

Jones sidestepped a charred body and continued down the street. What was once a church on his right was now a burned-out husk, with only a single spire that twisted upward. He paused, feeling some kind of pull to investigate further. Jones stopped short of the entrance, reached into his satchel, and sprinkled a handful of ash in front of him. Then he closed his eyes and wiped some on his face.

"Give me yesterday's sight," he whispered beneath his handkerchief.

With fists clenched, he took a deep breath through his nostrils and opened his eyes. No longer were his eyes staring out at the remains of the town, but at the church as it once was, engulfed in flames. He steadied himself as screaming fiery figures rushed all around him. People died in the pews as others tried to crawl over them, to no avail. Everywhere he looked, there wasn't man nor beast that the fire hadn't consumed. He glanced over his shoulder at the street, filled with people falling to their death, burned alive into statues of charcoal.

And then suddenly, the roar of the fire hushed to the sound of a whisper.

"Jacob," it called him by name.

He turned and stared at the burning pulpit, flames licking up the spire.

"Jacob," it called again.

Through the flames, a dark figure walked across the dais and past the pulpit, as the back of the church fell to the ground. Covered in inky blackness from head to toe, it dragged an arm, withered, old, and bleeding with a slave's chain on its wrist.

"Who are you?" Jones stammered.

The Inky Figure turned to him. Its teeth chattered over a low moan, and its murky, blood-red eyes met his.

"This is not your battle," the Figure said. "Your gift will not prevail."

"How do you know this?" Jones responded.

The figure raised its arms. The flames gathered around it like an unholy shrine.

"Our time has not yet come, Jacob," the Figure spoke. "But know you this: no chain of man can bind my wrath. Death to him that crosses my path."

And then it turned, walking toward the fire, leaving a trail of dark blood in its wake.

"How do you know my name?" Jones shouted.

The Figure paused, keeping its back to him and then laughed wickedly.

"How do you not know mine, Jacob Jones?"

The Figure walked into the fire, consumed by the flames, until there was nothing but fire. And then the fire itself disappeared with the fading sun.

"Jones?" Odessa called from behind him.

He stared off into the badlands as the sun faded over the hillside. She dismounted and tied their horses to a charred post. She approached him slowly. She circled Jones, but he looked right through her, as if she wasn't even there. She reached out and touched his face.

"Jones, what's wrong?" She wiped the ash from his face.

Jones blinked as if coming out of a trance. He looked down at Odessa, her eyes filled with concern and a twinge of fear.

"Something I saw," he said. "Something dark and—"

"—And what?"

He struggled to process it all. He scanned around, seeing the town just as they found it, dead and burned. He bent down and grabbed a handful of dirt and held it out to Odessa.

"Tell me what you see," he asked.

She looked into his hand and studied the soil.

"Just dirt," she replied. "What do you see?"

He took her hand and held the dirt before her again.

"And now?"

Odessa slowly looked at his hand again. Her eyes widened. Now she saw the blood.

"What does it mean?" she asked.

Jones brushed the dirt away. The blood was no longer visible to either of them.

"It means we need to get back to Menifee."

He took her hand and started off, but Odessa pulled back.

"This is the first time I've seen you afraid, Jones. Why?"

He gently tugged for her to keep moving and led her over to mount her horse. Try as he might, Jones could not find the words to tell her what he'd seen. He didn't know how to describe the eerie warning he'd been given or how, for the first time in his life, doubt had found its way into his head. A nagging doubt that what was coming for Menifee was something that he didn't understand—at least not yet. He searched his heart as he stared into Odessa's eyes. Despite how desperately he wanted to share what he'd learned with her, he didn't know how to say it. His eyes fell as he took his horse's reins and mounted up again. Odessa frowned, confused at the despair on Jones's face.

"Quail!" he shouted, "I've seen enough."

They rode hard back to Quail and then the three of them rode out of Gilly Pines as if they'd seen the devil himself. As he whipped his horse, riding fast, Poole's dark warning echoed in Jones's mind.

"The blood, Jones."

***

Night had long since fallen by the time they returned to Menifee. Though the toll on their bodies wasn't evident, the grave looks on their faces said so much more. Jones and Quail pulled up to the Sheriff's office as Odessa paused a few feet behind them.

"Quail, go see Doc Willis and find out how Sheriff Poole is doing," Jones ordered.

"Yes, sir." Quail turned his horse and trotted off.

Jones dismounted and tied off his horse as Odessa moved up beside him. He smiled as she looked down at him.

"I appreciate your help, Miss Odessa," Jones thanked her.

"You keep your feelings close, Jones," Odessa spoke. "But your face speaks aloud."

Jones grinned. "What does it tell you now?"

Odessa tightened her grip on her reins and gazed deeply into his eyes. She sensed something kindred in his brown eyes, something that took the words from her lips. It was a strange sensation for a woman who was used to speaking her mind. She turned her horse, but kept her eyes on him.

"You'll have need of me again, Jones," she told him.

Before he could respond, she rode off, passing Quail as he returned.

"That's a might powerful woman," Quail reflected.

Jones grunted in response as they watched Odessa disappear out of the light of the lanterns on main street, and into the night.

Jones sighed, "I need to speak with the men you and Poole rode with to Gilly Pines."

"You think they know something about what happened to Sheriff Poole?"

Jones peered at the saloon and grumbled as he brushed off his badge. "Somebody does."

As he crossed the street, Jones noticed a tiny figure moving past the saloon. It was Willa Stanton. She turned and smiled at him, just as before and just as chilling. Quail watched Jones grimly before he found the courage to follow.

Inside the saloon, an odd combination of whiskey, perfume, and piss filled the air. Pinecones hung near the door, which mildly masked the pungent aroma. A few scant patrons enjoyed an evening sip or a bowl of stew. Some were fresh off the trail, others were more permanent fixtures. None of them were ready for Jones to join them. As they stared in mute affect, the only audible sound was the faint wind. One man dropped his glass at the sight of Jones wearing the badge.

Jones made his way to the bar and leaned in with his hat dipped low. John Yeager, the balding bartender, was the first to greet him. Yeager was a burly man with arms still youthful from having lifted many crates of booze regularly. He worked a rag into a glass as Jones dug into his pocket and dropped a few coins on the bar.

"Whiskey, please," Jones requested.

Yeager kept working the rag without a word, glaring hard at Jones.

Quail finally arrived and slid up next to Jones.

"Yeager." Quail tipped his hat.

"Deputy." Yeager replied.

Quail swallowed hard as Jones and Yeager gave each other dark stares.

He finally mustered the courage to speak. "Well, now, I believe the man ordered a drink."

Surprised by Quail's gumption, Yeager set the glass down and hoisted a bottle on the bar.

"Much obliged," Jones thanked him.

"Not accustomed to having a colored at my bar," Yeager said. "Especially not one with a badge."

"Since I ain't never been here," Jones poured himself a drink. "It's a first for us both."

Jones passed the bottle to Quail, who declined.

"Where's Sheriff Poole?" Yeager inquired.

Joneses eyes fell on Quail. "This ought to be entertaining," Jones muttered to himself.

Quail grabbed the bottle and downed a stiff drink. He wasn't much of a drinker, so he almost heaved, but managed to keep his feet beneath him.

"Sheriff Poole took ill," Quail turned toward Jones. "This here's our new sheriff."

Behind them, a group of men suddenly rose from their seats, their drinks crashing to the floor.

A man called out, "The hell you say, boy?"

Jones turned slowly, the man's words striking a sour chord. He dropped his hand to his gun. His fingers danced on the hilt.

"His name is Deputy Quail," Jones replied.

The man stepped out and showed his own gun. "That badge don't make me no mind, nigger. I don't take shit from your kind."

Jones lifted his glass to his lips and slowly finished his drink.

"Best use that mouth to breathe with while you still can, Mister," Jones warned calmly.

The man took a fighting stance, ready to draw on Jones.

"Come on then, boy!" the man raged.

"Say it one more time," Jones stood erect. "You'll die with your eyes open."

A hush fell over the saloon. All eyes watched Jones and the man make their stand, a frozen moment before one of them would die. But before all hell broke loose, a small but defiant voice called out.

"Wait! Stop!" Anna Hanks rushed into the saloon.

She marched right between Jones and the man. She hadn't made so much as a peep since her ordeal on Jones's first day in Menifee. She had a slight scar near her mouth, which made her seem even more determined to be heard. Her eyes fell on Jones first.

"You're the one who saved me and my little girl, Mister," Anna announced loudly.

"Yes, Ma'am," Jones nodded and kept one eye on his adversary.

"And you run that no-good husband of mine out of town."

Jones nodded again.

"Well, I don't care if you were pink polka dotted with bells on!" She lifted her chin defiantly, marched up to Jones, and held out her hand. "You saved me and my baby girl. We owe you our lives. I never got to thank you proper. Thank you."

Jones extended his hand to her. Anna grabbed it and blessed him with kisses over his knuckles. This took Jones and everyone else by surprise. Anna wiped a tear from her face and beamed at him.

"Anything at all you need, you don't pause to ask, you hear?" her voice trembled.

"Thank you kindly, Ma'am."

Anna took in the badge, then glared at the man on the other side of the confrontation.

"Law says any man draw on the Sheriff, we hang 'em," she turned to Quail. "Ain't that right, Deputy?"

Quail jumped up beside Jones. Inspired by Anna's proclamation, he puffed his chest out like a proud peacock.

"Yes, Ma'am. On the books," Quail confirmed.

Anna turned back to Jones. "Bring your horses by the livery. I'll make sure they get fed proper and see to it your belongings are stored."

And with that settled, Anna hefted her skirt and marched out the door. Suddenly aware that everyone in the salon had abandoned him, the man humbly removed his hat and nodded respectfully at Jones.

"Beg your pardon, Sheriff," he said. "Meant no disrespect."

Jones nodded as the man slinked back to his friends. Jones patted Quail on the back as they returned to the bar where Yeager had already filled their glasses. Jones raised his glass to Quail.

"Quail, I do like the women in this town," Jones threw his drink back.

Eleven

In the Sheriff's office the next morning, Quail's leg quaked nervously as he stood next to Jones, sitting in Poole's chair. Before them were the riders who first went to Gilly Piles and discovered tragedy. Bob Meachum, a rancher; Early Porter, a shop owner; Sam Crisman, a farmer; Ned Reed, a handyman; and the portly Gabe Waller, all bristled at the sight of Jones wearing Poole's badge and occupying his chair.

"Poole wanted me to head off whatever you saw in Gilly Pines," Jones informed them. "But frankly, before. I need your help."

Porter responded first. "Help how?"

"Anything you might remember from the town, something not quite right," Jones added.

"You mean like a town full of burned bodies?" Meachum piped in.

"Especially that," Jones replied.

"We figured whoever did it burned them where they be," Crisman joined in.

Jones chewed on this for a moment. "And the people in the livery?"

The men look at each other, dumbfounded.

"I don't get your meaning," Waller said.

"I mean what Sheriff Poole found in the livery in Gilly Pines."

Jones was quick to catch the flash of recognition that washed over all their faces. They indeed knew something.

"Poole said Quail found more bodies in the stable," he continued. "Too many to count. Burned so badly that they fused together, no beginning and no end to distinguish them. According to Poole, every single one of them was burnt to a crisp."

The men avoided Jones's eye contact, exchanging sideways glances and fixing their eyes on the floor. Sturdy men like this had probably done everything they could to forget and never spoke of it again. No doubt the gruesome remains of Gilly Pines still haunted their dreams.

"I reckon if it was like any other stable, plenty of straw and other kindling that should have gone up with them," Jones surmised. "My question, gentlemen, how's it not a single strand of hay caught fire, but all the people did? And why was the fire that burned the people different from what set their buildings on fire?"

The weight of this revelation made them all look up at him, and a quiet gasp escaped Reed's lips. The horror of it was in each of their eyes—*how did Jones know?*

"Poole told us to burn it down. H-he told us not to take a thing from Gilly Pines," Reed finally spoke.

"And is that what happened?" Jones asked darkly.

Again, the men suddenly became mute, a telling silence that only brought more dread.

"I didn't take nothing!" Meachum exploded.

"Weren't me, I'll tell you that!" Porter exclaimed.

The other men grumbled and nodded in agreement. Jones studied them with a harsh grimace, but he found no lies in their eyes. No intent or fear that they had something to hide. Jones crossed his arms, annoyed. Had he guessed wrong? Maybe it wasn't any of these men. But then, the sound of Quail anxiously shuffling from one foot to the other caught ear. He spun his chair slowly to the young deputy. His heart sank, and all eyes fell on Quail as he stood there biting his nails.

"Deputy?" Jones's eyebrows raised.

"It was cold that night." The words cracked in Quail's throat. "J-just an old blanket. H-help keep me warm on the way back. I didn't think—"

"—You ignorant sum bitch!" Meachum yelled.

"Enough," Jones barked, as he looked up at Quail. "Where is it?"

With a somber look, Quail led them back to his sleeping quarters. It was an austere, rectangular room, and in the corner, a makeshift bed with not much more than a tac for a mattress. Laying atop it was a bronze-colored blanket with an indigenous diamond pattern, definitely Choctaw. It was a harmless-looking thing, adorned with symbols at both ends.

"Here it is," Quail confessed.

Jones moved past the others and picked up the blanket. He held one hand over the blanket and closed his eyes. Through the murky darkness, he saw the image of a village of Choctaw people. A tranquility washed over Jones. A deep sense of peace emanated from every person he envisioned. The community lived in harmony, with each other and with the land. All seemed idyllic until... fear. Unimaginable fear consumed them. A putrid, acrid darkness covered the sky. Thunder rolled in ever-deepening waves, driving them all to their knees. And when it seemed they couldn't bear more, then came the fire, which, more than anything, shook Jones to his core. The scene resembled a horrific sensory memory from his own past, except it played out on people he'd never known. Wide eyes and shrieks, running as though death itself chased them into oblivion. Their panic and terror were more than familiar.

Quail quietly watched him, listening as Jones murmured in a language he couldn't quite cipher. Under his breath, the trembling deputy whispered his own prayer. Jones stepped back, opening his eyes.

"I-Is there evil in it?" Quail's voice quivered.

Jones shook his head. "It didn't come from this."

"S-so, what do we do now?" Quail asked.

Jones turned back to the men, eyes filled with every shade of dread and concern. How could he begin to explain the hellish door they may have opened? Jones wondered if even he could stand against such an evil.

"The negro folk," Jones said, "see if they got any Black Tomatoes. Get a couple over to Doc Willis."

"What do you want us to do?" Meachum piped in.

For the second time, Jones didn't have an answer.

***

Jones had sternly instructed the others to keep what they'd learned to themselves to avoid causing further confusion amongst the townsfolk, but even he doubted that such a thing was possible, being as skittish as the men were. He spent most of the day trying his best to reassure folks and go about the everyday business of being sheriff, until he could work out what to do to protect Menifee from the fate of Gilly Pines. Thankfully, the most excitement he had was settling an argument between two women about whose pie tasted best. Anna Hanks stopped in with lunch for Quail and Jones, relaying a message from Doc Willis that Poole was improving, albeit slowly. When the mayor and the minister paid a brief visit, Jones kept Quail busy tidying the jail. They hoped to get inside information about his plans, but since he wasn't yet certain himself, they left emptyhanded.

Near sundown, he carried a plate of food and quietly made his way to the livery stable, weary and worn from the events of the last few days. He tried to eat, knowing he'd be better for the nourishment, but he had no appetite. Jones meticulously settled his horses down for the night and hung their saddles over the stalls. He whistled while he worked, trying to settle his own nerves.

Maybe it was the numerous visions he'd experienced recently or his concern for Poole that kept him on edge. A snap of hay underfoot suddenly caught his ear and made him step over to his gun belt. He whistled louder as he reached under a blanket and grabbed one of his guns. He whirled, pistol in hand, and dropped to the ground when he saw Odessa standing in the light of a candle.

"Miss Odessa," he stammered.

"Thought you might be hungry." She stared at him, wondering why he was on the ground. "But perhaps you and your gun need a moment."

Jones frowned, lowering his gun. "Quail's wife brought me some food a while ago."

Odessa spied the half-eaten meal in front of a stall. A smirk crossed her lips.

"Miss Helen's a good woman, except in the kitchen," Odessa explained. "Most white folks don't care for her food, let alone colored."

"That right?" He grinned and put his gun back.

Odessa smiled. "We were hoping you'd join us."

"We?"

Moments later, Odessa guided Jones to the back of the stable, where scores of Brown and Black people had gathered. The Choctaw and the former slaves of Menifee, dark and distinctive faces that had borne more ungracious grief than anybody has a right to. But tonight they smiled. In joyous earnest, some spirit-danced in the way of their elders, while others shuffled and clapped to the sound of a fiddle and a beating drum. There were makeshift tables and a row of large stew pots bubbling over an open fire. It was a sight Jones had never seen. Jones smiled, watching as men, women, and children found reason to dance. For most, it was their first taste of freedom. And as he and Odessa entered the scene, each of the adults took a moment to shake Jones's hand. Jones wasn't accustomed to this either.

"This is their way of thanking you," Odessa explained.

"Law did that," Jones replied. "Not me."

"Still, they are grateful for you," Odessa took his hand. "We all are."

He followed the smile in her voice to the one on her face, a warmth he hadn't seen in a dog's age and never at him. Jones tracked how the people seemed drawn to Odessa, reaching for her with a sense of reverence, acknowledging her, it seemed, even more than most of the elders.

"They seem to take a shine to you," Jones noted.

"Women have always led the people," Odessa beamed. "It is our way."

An old man walked up to Jones and handed him a cup of sour mash.

"Drink, drink," the old man spoke in the Choctaw language.

Jones took a sniff and thought better of it. "Much obliged."

Odessa spoke to the man in their language. "He does not speak our words, Elder."

But Jones responded, "Chahta iskitini anumpuli li."

Odessa gasped in delighted astonishment. "You speak our language?"

"Like I said, a little," Jones smiled.

The old man waited for Jones to take a taste. Eventually, he brought the cup to his lips and sipped. Despite his best effort to be gracious, he cringed. The old man smiled widely, showing he was missing a few teeth. Jones sipped some more of the mash for the elder's benefit. Satisfied that Jones was enjoying the drink, the old man teetered away.

Odessa studied Jones, especially his uniform.

"You kill many natives for them?" she frowned.

"Not in the war I fought," he replied. "Men I killed were white men."

"Yet you wear their colors," Odessa pointed out.

"Better than their chains." His eyes met hers.

"And still, you fight for them." She steeled her gaze.

"I fight..." he paused, choosing his words carefully. "For something else."

"Still, for them."

Jones shakes his head, pointing up to the sky. "For Him."

Odessa trailed his gaze upward, into the star-filled night sky. In that moment, she understood Jones paid heed to an authority greater than any human. She saw him in a much different light. Not so much a former slave and soldier who'd become a healer, but a man whom hatred had not scarred and left empty. A man for whom violence and bigotry hadn't turned into a bitter version of what he was meant to be. Indeed, he was so much more.

"So, the spirits favor you, Jones," she grinned.

"Jacob," he said. "That's my first name."

"I like it better than Black Bones," she admitted.

"Name came with the calling." His eyes met hers again.

She nodded, considering the spiritual burden he carried, and turned her attention to those celebrating.

"Our struggles seem to have led us on similar paths," Odessa sighed.

Jones looked out over the group. He noted that some of them were like Odessa, the product of mixed parents. Something in their eyes drew him deeply.

"That how your people came to be among mine?" Jones asked.

"Some of your people ran to mine, in search of freedom from chains," she gazed out at the celebration. "Some became my people."

Jones nodded. "Strength in numbers."

"The strength is not our numbers, but in our blood," Odessa stretched out her hand. "The spirits favor both our people. Blessing is in our veins. Great is the blood of two... as one."

"Least yours had a choice," Jones lamented.

Odessa turned back to him. The sadness in his voice struck a familiar heartache within her.

"None of us had choices, Jacob."

"I reckon you'd be right," he admitted.

Jones connected deeply to the anger in her words. His people were stolen from their homeland and sold into forced labor with no hope of freedom or autonomy, not even over their own bodies. But Odessa and her kin had their land—their home—ripped away from them through worthless treaties and empty promises. Foreign diseases and new weapons cost the countless lives of Odessa's people. And with the westward push, their children were forced into white education, no longer permitted to speak their own language or practice their own traditions. Their very existence was being erased. It was a weight he himself barely understood.

"Master. Slave. Hero. Villain," Odessa surmised. "It always comes back to who speaks these words, to whom tells the tale, and even then…"

Her words trailed off as she turned her eyes away from him. Her people had endured these unjust atrocities long before Jones' ancestors set foot on the land. In Odessa, he felt a century of agony wrapped in the sweetest voice he'd ever heard.

"You know," Jones changed the subject, "I'm getting powerful hungry. I don't suppose there's some honey to go with that fried chicken?"

Odessa's smile returned. She took his hand and guided him to a table.

"You're a peculiar man, Mr. Jones," she said.

"Funny people keep telling me that," he smiled.

Odessa grinned back. "I like peculiar things."

"That a fact?"

There was something in her touch that made Jones's heart feel light, as if he could float on air. As her fingers locked with his, all the cares of the last few days seemed to peel away in the evening breeze. Was this what freedom felt like?

But the moment would be short-lived when a young Black child collided with Odessa.

"Miss Odessa," he exclaimed in a panicked voice. "Please, come quick!"

Jones clocked the fear in Odessa's eyes. The feeling of joy drained from every pore in his body, replaced again by the dread he'd carried with him since the day his gift manifested in his life. And though it was Odessa they called upon, he knew the call would be his to answer.

TWELVE

These dark happenings were becoming more and more frequent in Menifee, foretelling that something was making its presence felt with greater strength each time. And with each occurrence, Jones realized that everyone in Menifee was running out of time. As Jones and Odessa followed the child around a corner, a woman ran past them, screaming. The few townspeople who were still out at this late hour backed away in horror, revealing a dark form in the middle of the street.

This time it was Meachum. He stumbled awkwardly down the street, careening toward Jones and Odessa. The street lanterns cast long shadows, but even so, they could see his face bore the same mark that Poole had. In his right hand was a blood-soaked axe. And in his left hand, he held the dripping head of Ned Reed.

"Sweet Jesus," Jones gasped.

He held his arm out instinctively to protect Odessa. From the left side of the street, Mayor Rodgers and his men emerged from the hotel. From the right, Quail barreled from the sheriff's office. All of them stopped and stared, as Meachum mumbled... in Choctaw.

"Meachum?" Quail stammered, reaching for his gun.

Meachum craned his neck oddly in the Deputy's direction, as if his head was off-kilter and somehow disconnected. His jaws moved, but his words became nothing more than guttural sounds.

"Great Mother," Odessa whispered beside Jones.

"Stay here," Jones ordered.

He marched forward, hand already reaching for the ashes in his satchel.

"Who are you, unclean one?" he demanded.

Jones dropped ash in Meachum's path. A clicking noise came from Meacham's throat as he staggered forward. Jones spread a line of ash between them in the dirt.

"Speak your name, demon," Jones shouted in his African tongue. "I command you!"

Meachum halted. His eyes glistened like silver pools in his head. He drew heavy, stuttering breaths, his chest heaving up and down. Ned Reed's head dropped from Meachum's hand and tumbled across the dirt, stopping short of Quail's feet. Quail fought back the urge to vomit. Suddenly, Meachum let out an unholy scream and charged at Jones, barreling through the ash that held no power over him. He raised the axe high, but Jones sidestepped it seconds before the axe came crashing down.

Jones threw a fistful of ash in Meachum's face and blinded him. Meachum swung wildly and hit Jones with a backhanded smack. Jones spun to the ground, lying face down in the dirt. Meachum raised the axe again. Jones quickly rolled to his left, this time escaping certain death by mere inches. Behind his head, Jones grabbed at Meachum's ankle in the dirt.

"Jones, behind you!" Quail screamed.

Jones yanked his ankle, flipping Meachum onto his back in the dirt. He kicked the axe away and scrambled over Meachum. He pinned him to the ground and chanted.

"Menifesini āsiralehu!" Jones shouted.

But Meachum somehow lifted Jones from him and threw him high in the air with inhuman force. Jones fell hard, a few feet away, left winded and dazed by the impact. Meachum clambered across the dirt to grab the bloody axe again.

"What are you?" Jones stammered.

Whatever he was, this wasn't Meachum anymore. Worse still, Jones seemed powerless to stop it. Meachum raised the axe and then—

BLAM! BLAM! BLAM!

Three shots struck Meachum's chest. He blinked down at his wounds, confused, then raised the axe again.

BLAM! BLAM! Two more shots.

Odessa turned to see Rodgers stepping into the street, his gun trained on Meachum. Rodgers steadied for another shot. Meachum staggered but didn't fall. Gentry stepped up beside Rodgers and unloaded on Meachum. A headshot finally toppled him. Odessa ran to Jones.

"Jacob!" she exclaimed, checking him over.

Dazed, Jones shook his head to clear away the cobwebs. His eyes came into focus on Meachum as he laid still, bleeding.

"What in God's name is happening?" Gentry shouted.

"It's not done." Jones pushed up to his knees.

To everyone's horror, Meachum sat upright. With a sinister smile, his face turned a ghostly white. He tilted his head back and let out a predatory, bone-chilling howl. Still on his knees, Jones's eyes turned coal black.

"Ingasa Hakana!" Jones commanded.

Meachum burst into flames, engulfed in fire from head to toe. He flailed like an animal caught in a trap, thrashing in all directions until he mercifully slowed and fell to the ground, finally dead.

Odessa struggled to steady Jones, whose eyes stayed on Rodgers and Gentry, their pistols still raised. Their faces were frozen with fear and astonishment. Quail hurried over to check Meachum's body.

"He's dead," he announced, perhaps to reassure himself more than any onlookers.

Quail stepped over to Jones and helped Odessa get him to his feet. Leaning on Odessa and Quail, Jones glimpsed Parson Greene, safely out of harm's way behind Rodgers and Gentry, sneering at him with an air of superiority. As people peered out windows and emerged from a few buildings, their eyes once again held mistrust and fear. What little confidence the town of Menifee had in Jones had evaporated, and if these shocking events somehow pleased any man, it was indeed Parson Greene.

Inside the hotel parlor, Odessa tended to Jones's wounds. As Rodgers and his men, including Parson Greene, returned to their seats, Quail tried to make a supportive stance on the other side of Jones. Several empty whiskey bottles littered the parlor tables. Rodgers brooded over a glass alongside Parson Greene.

"I seen this in a vision," Greene pointed at Jones. "The Lord showed me this man would bring darkness upon us."

"I fear sermons won't help us, Parson," Rodgers lamented, tipping back his drink.

"We need to have faith, Mayor," Greene implored. "Faith in The Lord!"

"I got faith in my Colt and a mess of bullets," Gentry added, glowering at Jones. "Definitely not in some colored speaking gibberish!"

"There must be a rational explanation for this," Rodgers said.

"Ain't no reasoning to what I seen," Quail added.

Now more accustomed to the taste, he held his whiskey like a man who was nursed on it. Odessa tended to the gash on Jones' head while he listened to them all speak.

"It has to be some kind of sickness," Gentry speculated.

"Ain't no sickness make a man take six bullets and keep coming," Rodgers rebuffed him.

"Somebody's gotta tell Reed's wife." Quail shook his head.

Gentry spun angrily at Quail. "You got the damn badge, Deputy! How come you ain't doing your job?"

"Leave him be," Jones finally spoke.

Gentry downed a shot and jabbed a finger at Jones. "All that talk about you saving this town and look at you. Your black ass nearly ended up like Reed!"

"Mr. Gentry—" Rodgers attempted to calm him.

"—Y'all seen it, plain as day!" Gentry shouted. "Meachum had him dead to rights! Where was his mumbo-jumbo then? Answer me that!"

All eyes fell on Jones. He inhaled deeply and exhaled, then slowly pushed Odessa's hand away.

"Did you happen to see him rise up after you shot him, Gentry?" Jones snapped back.

Even Rodgers stopped mid-sip at the realization of this. Gentry stood speechless.

"However fickle you all may be," Jones stated, "Poole crossed four states to find me. He brought me here to stop whatever evil was about to lay hands on this town."

"Admirable as that may be, Gentry does have a point," Rodgers fired back. "Your tricks seemed no match for Meachum."

"He's a huckster, if you ask me!" Gentry blurted out.

Jones glared long and hard at Gentry. Then he closed his eyes and murmured to himself.

"Well, boy?" Gentry grew louder. "What ya got to say for yourself?"

Jones stood up and limped over to Gentry, meeting him square on, eye-to-eye.

"On the off chance that you were struck blind every time I fought the darkness that's befell this town," Jones gritted, "Allow me to show you personally, some things ain't beyond my ability to discern."

Jones grabbed Gentry's hand. Gentry tried to pull away, but couldn't.

"The day your momma died, you cried three straight days. Your pappy took you out to learn how to shoot when you were ten, and that's how you got that scar between your fingers."

Jones dropped Gentry's hand, leaving him speechless. Next, Jones limped over to Parson Greene and did the same.

"And Parson, you been fawning over Mr. Rodger's niece, telling her of your affections for two years now. She's getting tired of waiting, too."

"How in God's name do you know that?" Greene stammered.

"Because the spirits favor him!" Odessa piped up.

Jones limped his way to Rodgers, who pulled his hands back, mea culpa.

"Count me satisfied by your demonstration, Mr. Jones," Rodgers supplanted.

Jones smiled and made his way back to Odessa. He laid a gentle hand on her shoulder.

"To answer your question, Parson, the same way I know what took hold of Poole, Meachum, and I suspect Reed, before he died," Jones explained. "Whatever it is, it ain't evil."

Odessa paled. "How do you know that?"

"Only way I can explain why nothing I did worked on either of them," Jones shrugged. "Ain't no evil stands up against what I can do. If'n it can, it can't be evil."

Rodgers ran his finger against the rim of his glass, curious.

"And what does all of that mean, exactly?"

Jones poured himself a glass of whiskey and gazed into it.

"After Hanks, I told Sheriff Poole there was more darkness here than he could imagine. But it ain't just come here." Jones threw his drink back. "It's always been here."

***

A saddle-weary Hanks barely kept himself upright. He leaned into his horse, nearly overcome with exhaustion. His lips were cracked and dry from days without food or water. A light in the distance ahead of him glimmered like a ray of hope as he came upon a campsite. The smell of pork and beans hit his nose as he struggled to focus on the firelight a few yards ahead.

"Merciful God, thank you," he rasped through tears.

As he entered the camp, he ungracefully slumped off his horse and fell to the ground. He didn't bother to dust himself off as he waddled forward. Hanks found himself in the presence of nine men—the Slavers that Poole and Jones encountered in Tennessee. They eyed him with intense suspicion.

"Beg pardon, friends," Hanks pleaded. "Might you have a plate for a weary traveler down on his luck?"

Collins looked him up and down, before he shoved a forkful of beans into his mouth, while a haggard Hanks wobbled in front of him. The smell of the food made Hanks's stomach grumble.

"I ain't got money to pay ya, but I'm a blacksmith by trade," Hanks stated sheepishly. "I can tend your horses."

Collins nodded to one of his men, who handed Hanks a small tin plate with beans and a hunk of dried pork.

"You're welcome to join us, Mister," Collins invited him in.

"Thank you kindly." Hanks plopped onto the ground.

"Name's Collins. Me and my men are rounding up derelict niggers and returning them to proper service."

Hanks scooped beans into his mouth, noticing a group of men and women behind them huddled together in chains.

"Dennis Hanks, a pleasure," he replied between gulps. "Ain't had a meal this good in days."

Collins's men chuckled at Hanks and refilled his plate.

"You get separated from your people along the trail, Mr. Hanks?" Collins asked.

Hanks wiped his mouth on his sleeve, carefully considering his reply.

"Sad to say, I've been done a terrible injustice," Hanks began. "I was accused of something I ain't done did. God as my witness."

"That right?"

"I was merely correcting my child, as ascribed by the good book," Hanks continued. "Spare the rod and all that."

Collins nodded and returned to his plate.

"You'd think my neighbors would have come to my aid instead of heeding the word of a colored man," Hanks lamented.

Collins's eyebrows rose with interest. "A colored man?"

Hanks sucked in breaths between gulps of beans. "Yes, sir."

"Why in tarnation they do that?" Collins queried.

"If ya ask me, that darkie put some kinda hex on them," Hanks stated.

"What about the law in your town?"

"You mean Sheriff Poole?" Hanks got out between bites.

Collins sat upright. "Poole?"

"Yeah, you know him?"

"We had the pleasure of meeting him a couple weeks back, traveling with his slave," Collins explained.

Hanks let out a hearty belly laugh. "Poole ain't never owned no slaves."

Collins rose and threw a dark look across the camp to his men. Hanks stopped mid-chew, not sure why Collins seemed upset suddenly.

"This colored man who wronged you," Collins sneered. "What he look like?"

***

Jones sat on the steps of the hotel. He drew shapes in the dirt with a stick: a circle, a triangle, infinity. Odessa slid down next to him, silently taking his hand. Her eyes met his, ever radiant and offering comfort.

"Something ain't right here," Jones said.

"Perhaps the spirits will guide you," Odessa encouraged him.

"Maybe they have and I just ain't been paying attention." Jones kicked a stone.

Rodgers emerged from the hotel and lit a fresh cigar. A billow of smoke rose above him.

"They're losing confidence in you," Rodgers stated. "That badge can offer but so much protection now."

"Faith is the Parson's job," Jones replied.

"He's no friend to the colored, even behind the cloth." Rodgers drew on his cigar.

"And you?" Jones asked.

"I'm a politician, Mr. Jones," Rodgers admitted. "The mood of the people serve as my tea leaves. Often their fears determine which way I must pitch my sails, so as to always come out victorious."

Jones kept scrawling on the ground. "You be a man of the people, then?"

"As it suits my own interests, yes."

Jones felt someone's eyes on him. He looked up and saw Willa Stanton watching them from across the road, a lantern in her hand. Her eyes locked tightly on Jones with that smile. The same damned smile that shook him to the core.

"You know, Mr. Mayor, Odessa here may have been right."

"How so?" Rodgers asked.

"It ain't you I need to be hearing."

Rodgers eyed him smugly as Jones got up and walked away. Odessa glared at Rodgers before she turned and followed Jones. Gentry emerged, joining Rodgers, who tracked Jones's movement down the street.

"We oughta do something about him," Gentry said.

"Patience is a virtue, Mr. Gentry." Rodgers tapped ash from his cigar. "We'll bide our time. Let him play his hand."

Gentry's gaze loomed in Odessa's direction. "What about the girl?"Rodgers grinned. "Maybe when this is all over, she'll make a fine pearl to warm my bed." Gentry chuckled heartily as they returned to the hotel.

***

Willa Stanton teetered back and forth in front of the post office, as though someone were singing her a lullaby. She beamed at the sight of Jones and Odessa approaching her.

"Why bless my soul," Willa smiled. "Have y'all come to see me home tonight?"

Jones exchanged odd looks with Odessa before removing his hat. "We'd be right honored if you allow us to see you on your way, ma'am."

Willa passed her lantern to Jones, then took his free hand, squeezing tight.

"I told them you were a good man for a colored," Willa noted. "Might even have been a gentleman if you were a white man."

Odessa barely kept a chuckle inside as Jones glanced in her direction. Willa took her arm too as they headed off.

THIRTEEN

The Stanton estate sat at the easternmost end of Menifee. Settled when the town was first formed, it was one of two grand homes that graced each end of town. The Stanton family were ranchers who'd made their fortune driving cattle from the north. The Menifees, after whom the town was named, were a wealthy family that plied their trade in the railroad.

Willa married into the Stanton family after Noble Stanton courted her two days after her sixteenth birthday. They fell in love and married before malaria took both of Willa's parents. Some said that it was the loss of her parents that changed Willa. Some said it was after her husband was killed trying to break a wild stallion. In either case, Willa never took another husband and never again spoke to anyone about either tragedy. Her only response to any query regarding her family was that they still lingered in the halls of her home.

Jones had never set foot in a mansion—not even as a child on the plantation—and from the look on the faces of Willa's servants, she'd never had a negro come through the front door before. No Choctaw had ever set foot inside the home, either. Odessa marveled at the furnishings and appointments. They both were astonished as Willa introduced them to each bauble and knick-knack she owned by name.

"Follow me, my dears."

Willa led them by candlelight down the hall, past several rooms. Eventually, they arrived at the drawing room. It had all the charm of the Antebellum age: heavy curtains that framed tall windows, white porcelain fixtures, and the scent of pine in the air. A servant poured tea for them as Willa glided to a great chair next to a grand fireplace. Willa pointed to a velvet cushioned chair for Jones and another across the room for Odessa.

"There now, everything in its place." She lifted her tea and sipped.

"Thank you for the tea," Jones said.

"I must say, this is the first time I've entertained a colored man in my home." Willa remarked with much delight.

Jones caught Odessa hiding another smirk.

"I'm mighty grateful," Jones sipped his tea. "Ma'am, when I first arrived, you told me someone has been expecting me."

"Oh yes, it was a wonderful day." Willa replied.

Jones glanced at Odessa again and breathed deeply. "Who did you mean, Ma'am?"

Willa's eyes sparkled, but her teacup trembled in her hand.

"Why, the people who've been here forever, child." Willa said.

"You mean the townsfolk?"

Her face turned ghostly white.

"No child, didn't you hear me?" Willa smiled oddly, head cocked, and turned slowly to Odessa. "The ones who have been here forever."

Odessa leaned back in her seat, suddenly filled with concern.

"Who are 'they,' Ma'am?" Odessa asked.

Willa sat her cup onto its saucer and put them aside on an ornately carved side table next to her. She opened her blouse as if the climate had suddenly changed in the room.

"I must say, I've not felt like this since I was a young woman in my prime."

She fanned herself as Jones and Odessa sat confused by her machinations. Willa stretched out her hand to Odessa.

"Child, will you help an old woman?"

"Of course."

Odessa set down her teacup and walked over to the widow. Willa seized her arm. Odessa's eyes turned bright white and her body stiffened. Jones jumped to his feet to help but—

"—Hold your place, Black skin!" Willa warned.

Caught between his fear and his fury, Jones eased back into his chair. He tried to slip his hand into his pocket.

"Your medicine will not bind us here," Willa said gravely. The room grew dark around them. A strange mist rose from beneath the marble floor and filled the room.

"There's no need to harm the woman," Jones urged.

"And none shall come to her," Willa proclaimed. "They will speak through her as they have through me all these years." Jones showed his empty hands and moved to the edge of the chair.

"I reckon you tried to speak to me through Poole," Jones surmised. "Guess he didn't take to it for some reason."

Odessa craned her neck to him and spoke as many dark voices. "He fought us."

"And Meachum?"

"His own darkness took him."

"They didn't understand," Jones tried to explain.

"White skins do not try," they responded through Odessa.

"Then help me understand." Jones stood up. "Why do you attack these people?"

"We did not draw blood first," Odessa channeled. "But we shed it."

Jones leaned back, confused. His eyes fell on Willa.

"I remember my friends as a child, so many of them," Willa began, tearfully. "They shared their life and their land with us."

"Until Menifee came," Odessa said darkly.

"The town?"

"Thaddeus Menifee." Odessa turned to Jones.

Without warning, a blinding light suddenly struck Jones. Everything around him swirled like a storm of sand. Voices mixed into a wailing chant. The gale force surrounded and tossed him back and forth like a leaf in a winter wind. They seemed to lift him up before they drove him down to his knees, as if he were being pulled into the earth itself. And then, as suddenly as it started, it stopped. When Jones opened his eyes, he was no longer in the drawing room of the Stanton estate. Jones stared into an open range. Fields rippled under a gentle breeze as a huddle of wagons came to rest at a flowing stream. Settlers, full of trepidation after venturing too close to the badlands, descended from the wagons for a respite alongside the water's edge.

"All these lands once belonged to the Choctaw," the voices emanated from Odessa.

From one of the wagons, Cole Stanton stood alongside his wife Noelle and their sons, Arthur and Noble. They listened to Thaddeus Menifee, the group's leader, who stood by his wife and their tiny daughter, Willa. Thaddeus was a formidable man, quite used to imposing his will upon everyone under the sound of his voice.

"He brought them to our home," Odessa's voice thundered.

Thaddeus Menifee waved his hand over the land, proclaiming his vision of a glorious town, one free of 'Indian savages.'

"We welcomed them with arms open."

Choctaw Indians, native to the land, rode into the fledgling Menifee with skins and trinkets to greet their new neighbors. In the early days, their help and generosity was welcomed, but as Thaddeus's influence and power grew, so did the hatred of the indigenous people.

"They first shed our blood."

Jones saw Thaddeus Menifee lead an angry group of men against the Choctaw. They cut them down, men, women, and children in broad daylight. Those who tried to escape were trampled mercilessly by horses.

"But stealing this land was not enough."

Menifee and his marauders tracked the trail of the Choctaw to another village, and hunted them back to the land where Gilly Pines was settled.

"Three villages. Slaughtered."

Thaddeus and his men didn't just kill them, they burned them from their homes. Those who fought back were burned alive.

Once again, Jones was swept up in a sea of voices and whirling wind until he found himself on the floor of Willa Stanton's home. Pain and trauma washed over his face as he pulled himself back into his seat.

"God in Heaven," Jones stammered.

"White man's God did not save us," Odessa spoke.

"I begged my father to explain to me why they had to die," Willa sobbed. "They were my friends. I loved them."

"The towns before... the massacres..." Jones pieced it all together.

"Their blood for our blood."

"Why now, after sixty years?"

"Because now is the time foretold!" Odessa shouted. "The door can be opened now."

"This is why they need you, Jones," Willa added. "You are here to guide their way home."

Jones stood up, speechless, completely thrown by this revelation. This ran far deeper than anything he could have imagined. And now, after learning of the tragedy hidden in the very soil of Menifee, of the atrocity that had come back to repay the town in kind, Jones struggled to comprehend that he himself was the key to undoing a great injustice. His coming to this town was no mere happenstance. He was destined to come here.

"Wait—" Jones stammered.

"Choctaw and Slave, Native and Moor," Odessa continued channeling. "The bond of two bloods. The son of slaves is the door."

"The son of slaves is the door," Willa repeated.

Suddenly, a whirlwind erupted between them and turned into a pillar of fire. Though the light was brilliant, the fire itself seemed to leave everything around it unscathed. Jones jumped back to shield his eyes from the blinding light. It kept him from intervening, as Willa released Odessa's arm and Odessa walked toward the flame.

"Odessa!" Jones screamed.

Odessa remained locked in a trance, captive to the voices of her ancestors, still tightly held by those spirits. Jones tried to move around the fire, to somehow get in front of her, but the flames grew too wide for him to run around, and the pillar moved to match his every step.

Willa became childlike, rocking back and forth, repeating "The son of slaves is the door," over and over.

Odessa began reaching for the flame.

"Shit," he cursed.

Jones jumped through the flames, running right at Odessa, and wrapped his arms around her. Together, they rolled on the floor, safely away from the fire. Jones looked back to see the pillar of fire fade into a single strand of light before it completely vanished. He checked Odessa to make sure she was uninjured.

"Jacob? What is happening?" Odessa blinked, confused.

Willa reached out to them. Her bony fingers lighted on Jones's shoulder and gave him a start. Tears glistened on her cheek, but a peaceful smile filled her face.

"The son of slaves is the door," Willa said.

She buckled, fainting back safely onto a massive chair, illuminated by the moonlight through the windows. Odessa collapsed against his chest with a sigh, but even as he felt the warmth of Odessa's breath upon his skin, Jones knew the danger was far from over.

Fourteen

It had been one of the longest nights in Jones' life. Not even the battles he fought at Antietam or Shiloh, campaigns that seemed endless, could match the toll on his spirit that this night had taken. After putting the widow into her bed, Jones accompanied Odessa back into town, until she insisted she'd be alright to make her way home.

Back at the livery, Jones felt relief at focusing on the present. Alone with just his thoughts, he took water to his horses and made sure they were comfortable for the night. He stepped in beside his favorite horse, Helena, a beautiful Friesian with a luxurious mane, tail, and forelock. The horse nuzzled him as Jones caressed the horse's face, stroking its high-set neck. He enjoyed these quiet moments, absent the sound of men's fears ever filling his ears.

But his respite was brief as the light from a lamp moved alongside the stable to the door.

"Jones?" Odessa called out in a loud whisper.

Jones slowly stepped out of the shadows, and the light danced off his bare chest. One hand held high to shield against the light, and the other held his shirt."

Thought you'd gone back to your people for the night," he replied.

Odessa smiled. The sight of him took her a moment to absorb. His muscles rippled beneath his dark skin. This was completely unexpected, but certainly not unwelcome. He looked intently at her as she approached, taking in her black hair brushed back. The sweet fragrance of jasmine enveloped him. She gazed into his eyes for a long beat before her fingers landed on the charred bones around his neck.

"Are they a symbol of your tribe?" she asked.

"I guess you could say that." His eyes followed her fingers. "It's all that's left of my forefathers before they were…"

His hand fell against hers, lingering longer than it should have.

"So they are always with you," she completed his thought.

There was something in her eyes that gave him pause, causing his words to get lost in his throat. A few rare times in his life, he'd known the comfort of a woman. Once in a saloon that cared little for the color of his skin and more for the color of the coin in his pocket. He'd felt that warmth and burning desire, but this was the first time he'd ever felt captivated by a woman, and never one quite like Odessa Grayfoot. He swallowed hard as he tried to compose himself again.

"With what's happening in town," he said. "You'd be safer with your people."

Odessa moved in closer, so close that the mulberry ribbon trim on her cotton dress brushed against his chest. She stared deeply into his eyes as she reached for the belt around his waist.

"I feel safe here," she whispered. "With you."

"I, ummm—well, I guess I..." Jones stammered, lost in her dark eyes.

"Jacob?"

"Yes," he answered dryly.

"Stop talking."

She blew out the lamp and softly pressed her lips against his. Without another word, she took him by the hand and led him into an empty stall. She took a blanket and laid it down over the hay. Jones could feel his heart beating wildly as she gently pushed him down to the ground. Her soft touch felt electric as she undressed him, revealing the strength and scars of his body to her.

Odessa smiled as she lifted her dress over her head. Her beaded earrings shimmered in the half-light of the moon. Jones could only marvel at her beauty. She took his hands to rest upon her breasts as she straddled him. She ran her fingers over the scars from torture and battle on his chest. His body arched to meet her, his hips driving up as she guided him inside of her. They gasped in unison as she brought the full weight of her body down on him, and he met her every move. Their passion intensified in waves as they crashed into one another.

This was more than just the mere act of sex between them, more than just flesh against flesh. There was a spiritual intimacy to it, something stronger than anything Jones had ever felt with another human being. It reverberated through him like a heavenly chorus, driving them deeper and deeper into each other. Beyond the intoxication of the skin, the pulsing unison of energy spiraled up their spines until their spirits collided like the sun and the moon, bursting into a million stars being born before their eyes.

And in Jones's eyes, that was exactly what happened. He stared in utter astonishment as the night sky above opened like a celestial flower in bloom and swirled above them. The night was painted with gossamer in every hue and color, like a canvass of God. Forces beyond comprehension moved powerfully through them and made Odessa's hair rise as if lifted by the wind. She held his face as they reached the peak of their passion. Jones stared into Odessa's eyes, watching them become pools of bright light that engulfed them, taking them to a height that only God alone knew.

Later, with Odessa in his arms, Jones stared up at the night sky he was more accustomed to, with stars twinkling through the broken boards of the roof. Odessa stroked his chest lightly as she listened to his heart beating. This was Peace, also something new to Jones.

"Jones," she whispered. "What is your name?"

"You just said it," he replied.

"No, not the name the white man gave you," she explained. "What name did your people give you when you were born?"

Jones chewed on this for a moment. It had been so long since he spoke it aloud he had to allow his memory to find purchase in his mind.

"My father called me his tiny hand," Jones said. "But my people gave me a name I didn't understand when I was a child. Later I came to know it meant something: protector, warrior, defender. They called me Adjani."

Odessa smiled. "Strong. I like it."

"What name did your people give you?" Jones asked.

"I am called Ai Ne Chi Hoyo Ohoyoh," Odessa spoke. "It means—"

"—She who is preferred above all others," Jones finished for her.

"You do know our words," Odessa smiled. "I like this too."

"Sounds like the kind of name you give someone who means a lot to you," Jones replied.

"Where will you go when this is over?" Odessa asked as her fingers danced on his skin.

"Been thinking about Mexico," he replied.

"Mexico is no good. They kill Indians for money," she rebuffed him.

Jones stroked her hair. "Where would you go?"

"North," she sighed. "Near Canada. To the places where the old tribes roamed."

"Through the badlands?"

"They are not bad for me." She leaned up and stared at him. "Not bad for you either."

His hand fell to the bones around his neck. For a moment, he pondered what could be.

"I still got unfinished business," he replied.

"What is more important than breathing the fresh air?" Odessa wondered aloud. "Roaming the plains as a free man?"

"Justice?" the word tumbled from his mouth.

Odessa sighed as she fell back onto his chest and draped her arm over his shoulder.

"Is that all you wish for your life, Jacob Jones?"

Jones felt the weight of her question hit harder than anything he felt in his life. He'd lived his entire life and never once wondered if there was more in this life for any man like him, any Negro who wore the chains or felt the sting of a whip. Or watched his family torn apart before his very eyes, dragged away, never to be seen or heard from again. How could he dare dream there could be more for him? He stroked her hair, cherishing their closeness.

"Kinda gave up wishing a long time ago. First time a man ever took a whip to my back. When they sold my kin. When I fought in the war. Dreaming ain't been easy, not when you wake up to this."

Odessa took his hands, brought them to her lips, and kissed them lightly. Her heart sank at the sight of the scars that covered his arms from years of brutality. She held his hands against her cheeks.

"Choctaw and slave," she said under her breath.

"Native and Moor," Jones added.

"Only your flesh was beaten, Jacob," Odessa said boldly. "Your spirit, they can never touch. They can never extinguish your fire."

Jones didn't say another word. He pulled her close, lips crushing against one another, and then pulled her beneath him as they made love once more.

Much later, with a winsome smile and a blanket wrapped around her, Odessa walked back to her people's part of the sleepy town. When the sun rose a couple of hours later, she awoke inspired to spend more time with Jacob. She packed a basket with berries, cornbread wrapped in husks for roasting, and some squash. She hurried back to town and convinced Deputy Quail to watch the sheriff's office so she could take Jacob to her favorite spot near a stream where the fish were plenty.

It took some coaxing, but Jacob obliged her request, and they enjoyed a beautiful day at the water's edge. He allowed himself to embrace this new Peace he felt with her, to laugh and to chase her in the water, to feel truly free. They spent time in each other's arms once more, getting to know every muscle, curve, and scar that they carried. It was a day filled with sunlight and birdsong, one that Jacob hadn't experienced before. Such frivolity was never part of a childhood within the bonds of slavery.

When Jacob could no longer keep his thoughts away from his duty as acting sheriff and the impending fate of Menifee, he insisted they return to town. Just as they reached the trees behind what was once the mansion of Thaddeus Menifee, Odessa grabbed Jacob and pulled him behind a tree to steal one last kiss while they still had some privacy. He was developing a deep appreciation for a woman who knows what she wants.

They parted ways near the sheriff's office. He stood outside the door and watched her until she disappeared into the golden purple sunset. It was a sight he'd never forget. When he stepped inside, it seemed Quail had gone to his quarters for the night, so Jones decided to make his way to the livery.

Odessa's feet had taken her nearly home, and all the while her thoughts lingered on Jones, his touch, his scent. So much so that her eyes were oblivious to the posse of ten men on horseback, barreling toward her. She gasped just as they pulled up before her, ominous and dark until she stared up at the face of Hanks glaring down at her.

"Her!" he shouted. "She was with him!"

Collins drew closer and leaned over his saddle, leering at Odessa.

"Young lady," he smiled. "You could save us a whole lotta trouble if you take us to that Black buck name of Jones."

FIFTEEN

N ot able to sleep, Jones stacked sacks of grain in his wagon. Across the way, a gingerly old codger tugged up his britches and watched Jones for a moment. Jones grabbed another sack to load, noticing the old man hoist his britches and runoff. *But what spooked him?*

Now Jones tensed, catching the stench of men fresh off the trail, a sour rotting lime smell that made him backtrack his steps. He reached into the wagon, but his guns were out of reach, hanging in the stall in the corner. The stench grew thick just as he laid his hand on an axe handle. The sound of someone sucking their teeth behind him drew his attention. Out of the corner of his eye, Jones saw the silhouettes of two men moving fast in his direction.

"Been looking for you, boy," the shorter man said.

Jones hid the axe handle behind him, waiting for them to make their move.

"Might be sorry you found me," Jones replied.

The taller man swung for Jones' head, but Jones easily leaned out of harm's way, tripping him as he fell forward. The shorter man charged. Jones jabbed the handle into his ribs and then swung in high, bringing it crashing into the man's head. Three more men appeared and surrounded Jones. He kept swinging wildly to keep them at bay. But behind him, Hanks crept up from the darkness. He smashed his gun into the back of Jones's head and knocked him out.

"Hot damn! That was some fun!" Hanks hooted.

Hanks directed the men to drag Jones up from the ground.

"Your black ass is mine now, boy," he spat. "Bring me those chains!"

Jones slipped in and out of consciousness as the sounds of wicked laughter trailed him into darkness.

***

At the sheriff's office, Quail stirred, awakened by a ruckus in the street.

"What in tarnation?" he muttered aloud.

He shuffled from his quarters to the front window to see men with torches tearing up and down the street on horseback.

"Sweet Lord!" he exclaimed.

He grabbed his rifle and bolted out the door.

Chaos reigned on Main Street as frightened people ran in every direction. Collins and his men terrorized anyone caught in their path. They nearly trampled a Black boy who darted back and forth, trying to find safety. A whip cracked at his back as he tumbled out of reach, safe behind an oak barrel. Not even a warning shot from

Quail could calm the madness. He jumped into the fray and bore down on Collins.

"Stop right there, mister!" Quail shouted.

Collins reared up his horse and sneered down at Quail.

"Son, don't you know help when you see it?" Collins shouted back.

"Ain't recall asking for help." Quail held his ground. "Who are you, and what are you doing here?"

"We've come to free you from the influence of a colored man," Collins replied.

"You mean Sheriff Jones?" Quail asked.

Collins's face reddened with rage. "What bedeviled you to make a nigger your sheriff?"

Angrily, Quail racked his gun and took aim at Collins.

"Mister, I don't know where you're from, but you best gather your men and go back the way you came."

Collins stared, dumbstruck. From their hiding places, the townsfolk gawked in silent awe, watching Deputy Quail defend his town with a courage none had ever seen from him before. Quail had come into his own and not a moment too soon. Collins sighed and took off his hat, shaking his head.

"Alright then, Deputy," Collins relented.

Then, in the blink of an eye, Collins shot Quail. BAM! First in the face, and then—BAM! BAM! BAM! BAM!—four more times. Someone screamed as Collins dismounted. BAM! He shot Quail a final time before he leaned over and ripped the badge from Quail's limp, bloody body.

"Race traitors don't deserve to wear no badge," Collins pinned it on himself. "This town needs white man's law!"

He got back on his horse while Hanks and his men dragged Jones into the street. Collins smiled at the sight of Jones.

"Yes indeed!" Collins exclaimed.

The mayhem in the streets reached Doc Willis's office where Poole lay. He was a far sight better but still recovering. He dragged himself upright, fighting the urge to vomit as he searched for his boots. After dressing himself as best he could, Poole wobbled out of Doc's office. He hung onto a beam, bracing at the destruction of life and property by Collins' men. They menaced anyone in sight and smashed anything in their way. In the center of town, they'd erected a massive wood pile and a stake.

"Sweet Jesus," Poole stammered.

One of Collins' men spotted Poole and whistled for his boss. Collins turned to see Poole stumble onto the street. He galloped hard at Poole and knocked him to the ground.

"Well now, how the mighty have fallen." Collins grinned.

"The hell are you doing in my town?" Poole weakly raged.

"It's my town now," Collins barked. "Thanks to you and that nigger, we've restored order to this place."

"You have no idea what you're doing," Poole looked around. "Quail? Where's my Deputy?"

Collins took off his hat, mocking reverence. "The good deputy has gone on to glory, where only God can forgive his transgressions. But you..." Collins signaled his men to grab Poole, "...You and your boy have a different destination."

It was a horrific sight: Jones, Odessa, and Poole tied at the stake with a pile of kindling at their feet, a throwback to a hundred-year-old nightmare reborn in the heart of Menifee. Townsfolk gathered, some frozen with fear and others out of morbid curiosity at the spectacle. They waited with wide eyes and fickle hearts for the bloodletting to begin. Collins held court before them all, a wretched regalia of unwashed slavers and those who stood with them. It was no surprise that Rodgers and his men found themselves among Collins' ranks. Never blind to an opportunity, Rodgers knew when to change horses in a race.

"Good people of Menifee!" Collins proclaimed like a politician himself. "My men and I have come to cleanse you of a pestilence that has beset your town. To save you all from the dark clouds that loom over you all."

He turned to see Jones, glaring and biting his lip.

"This man bedeviled your sheriff and tried to destroy your way of life."

"Liar!" Odessa screamed.

"He and this half-breed whore conspired to harm one of your own."

Collins pointed at Hanks, who stood there gloating as he waved a torch in front of Jones.

Anna jumped out of the crowd, seething with rage. "You got right no right to do this!"

"You get your ass back home, woman," Hanks jabbed a finger in her direction. "I'll deal with you soon enough."

Tearfully, Anna turned to Jones. "May God forgive us."

Anna glared at Hanks scornfully, understanding she was out muscled, before she disappeared into the crowd again.

"We mean to cleanse this town," Collins raised a torch. "With Holy Fire!"

Some of the townsfolk grumbled, but slowly, others agreed.

"Don't listen to him," Poole begged. "You people know me! I brought this man here to save us all!"

It was Rodgers who now stepped up, torch in hand.

"Do we know you anymore, Sheriff? Ain't you the same man who let this negro force me to give up my slaves?"

"The war ended that," Poole snapped at him. "You were just too stubborn to grasp it."

Collins turned to Rodgers. "What say you, brother? Is he right? Is this man some savior?"

Rodgers glared at Jones, triumphant. "I'll see him dead before I ever admit that."

"And so you shall, my friend," Collins smiled. "And so you shall."

Willa Stanton moved untouched through the mob, getting close enough to Jones to meet his eyes.

"But you promised you'd help!" she wailed and wept.

"Ma'am, his lies won't hurt anyone when we're done with him," Collins assured her.

But as Willa looked at Collins, her confusion turned to a furious glare.

"You came here to burn, child," Willa pointed at Collins and then his men. "All ya, burn!"

Collins chuckled and then laughed out loud.

"I believe you are correct, Ma'am," Collins hefted his torch. "I most definitely came to burn."

SIXTEEN

—·—

Collins threw his torch on the kindling surrounding Jones, sparking a small fire.

"Light 'em up boys!" Collins shouted.

A wave of torches flung through the air and landed in front of Jones, Odessa, and Poole. In seconds, the kindling ignited, and the flames grew quickly and ferociously.

"Burn nigger!" Hanks shouted.

As the flames devoured everything in its path, Poole gazed over at Jones with a sorrowful look as tears ran down his face.

"Jones!" he cried out. "I'm sorry. I didn't mean for this to happen."

Jones nodded at him and pulled hard against his chains, but to no avail.

"Ain't for you to apologize," he shouted back.

Jones turned to Odessa, head high and stone-faced. She refused to give their captors the satisfaction of crying out.

"We'll get out of this!" Jones yelled.

But instead of fear, Jones saw something else in Odessa's eyes. Clarity.

"Jones! The bond! We are the bond!" she shouted at him. "You are the door!"

Flames whooshed up high between them. Some of the townsfolk fell to their knees. Others wailed in an unholy chorus, as Collins laughed the laugh of the damned.

"Choctaw and Slave!" Odessa screamed to Jones.

Poole hung his head and whispered a last prayer. Jones locked eyes with Willa, crying with her hands holding her face. Suddenly, Odessa's voice reached him, and for him now, clarity.

Before his spiritual eyes, Jones witnessed more than just the secret of Menifee. He saw all the atrocities against the Indigenous people. Slaying and slaughter that led back to the foundation of the nation. He watched as Choctaw welcomed strangers with open arms, then cut down and their blood soaked the land. And then he saw the ships.

Ships crammed with Black men and women. He saw them dragged from their homes, many dying before they reached American shores. Next, he saw the fateful night that changed his life. The terrifying Dark Figure, and his younger self fighting to save his beloved mother. Then he saw his mother's pride and love for him in her eyes, and with her last breath, she whispered something sacred. The same words he'd heard days ago from Odessa and Willa Stanton. Words that would again change his life forever.

"Native and Moor," Jones remembered.

Ferocious flames danced at his feet and singed his boots. Even as his fate seemed inevitable, Jones finally understood what it all meant and what his role must forever be.

"I am the door!" Jones heaved.

The fire heated the chains around his wrists until they glowed orange, but Jones's skin remained untouched.

"I AM THE DOOR!" Jones screamed.

A bolt of lightning streaked from the sky amid Jones and Odessa, and a clap of thunder shook the ground beneath them. Jones' eyes rolled back, turning coal black. His head snapped back as the wind howled all around them. Collins' men struggled to control their horses. A dust cloud rose and blotted out the night sky. Odessa began chanting. Poole shut his eyes tight. He knew far too well what was coming. Collins barely held onto his bucking horse, bewildered.

"It's him! He's doing it! Shoot him!" Hanks pointed at Jones, screaming.

Collins wasted no time in turning his gun on Jones and firing.

BLAM! BLAM! He fired. But his bullets never found their mark.

"Shoot him!" Collins screamed.

A wailing howl spiraled around them like a dark choir, as his men fired wildly at Jones. The flames began to engulf Jones, but they didn't burn him. Collins, his men, and all the townsfolk froze, as Jones and the flames became as one. Jacob Jones was a man of fire. He raised his hands, and the chains melted from him.

In the language of the Choctaw, Jones called out. "Rise, brothers, come home at last."

No one could believe their eyes as three ethereal forms leaped from Jones and emerged with a Choctaw warrior's battle cry, dragging the flames with them in their wake. With ghostly arrows and tomahawks, they laid siege to Menifee.

Again, Jones shouted in Choctaw, "Rise, sisters, come home!" More ghosts exploded from Jones' chest. Women with spears of vengeance bore down on one of Collins' men. They impaled him and raised him high as his body caught fire.

"Mother of God!" Rodgers stammered in terror. Rodgers and his men ran in all directions. Collins' men fired frantically at anything that moved. Some fell, only to be scalped as their bodies ignited and burned.

Only Willa was one of the few passed over. She fell to her knees in a tearful, joyous release.

"I knew you'd come back!" she cried.

On the stakes, Odessa's bonds fell away, and she jumped to free Poole, pulling at the ropes around him. "Open your eyes, Poole! Bear witness to what happens here!"

"Get me outta this and I'll do more than watch!" he screamed.

She grinned as she set him free. "Good to have you with us again, Poole."

Jones leapt to the ground. Another crack of thunder shook the ground, and white lightning lit up the sky behind him. Flames covered him like a cloak imbued with a supernatural power only he could harness. He rose and staggered toward Collins, who kept shooting. BAM! BAM! BAM! Jones bore down on him, unharmed.

"Die, damn you! Die!" Collins screamed.

Collins' horse fearfully bucked and threw him to the ground. He scrambled to get to his feet as Jones marched toward him, picking up a pair of shackles from the ground.

"You can't kill me!" he yelled.

Jones gazed down at the shackles, which were covered in fire. He threw them at Collins. They locked around his wrists, searing into his flesh. Jones stood over Collins, who fell to his knees, screaming.

"You gave me to the fires." Jones grabbed him by the throat and lifted him high off his feet. "I give them back to you."

He writhed in agony, shrieking, as the fire leapt from Jones to engulf Collins. His neck exploded into flames that swirled around his head, and his body convulsed under Jones's grip. For Collins, seconds may have well been like a million years as he died slowly. Every part of him was incinerated into smoldering ash, except for the sheriff's star. It spun like a top, then landed right side up next to his ashes.

The townsfolk found themselves caught in the crossfire between a hail of bullets and spirits of vengeance. Those who didn't align themselves with Collins and Rodgers managed to avoid both the gunfire and the righteous flames. Poole leapt down to earth, tried to get his bearings when a voice called to him.

"Sheriff Poole!" Anna shouted.

Off to his left, Poole saw Anna running at him, shotgun in hand. She threw it in his direction and raised another. He'd never been so happy to see her in his life.

"God bless you, Anna!" Poole thanked her.

She flanked Poole, shooting one of Collins' men in the face and knocking another off his horse.

"He did bless me!" Anna shouted back. "With good aim!"

Poole racked the rifle and aimed at another rider. He clipped him in the shoulder and fired another round to his face. Odessa tumbled forward and picked up a gun from one of the fallen. She took out one of Rodgers' men and another rider.

"Good shooting, Odessa!" Anna congratulated her.

Odessa smiled at Anna as they marched with guns blazing. They moved in unison, like glorious Amazons, cutting down any man fool enough to get in their way. When Anna ran out of ammo, she flipped her grip on the rifle and used the stock to break the jaw of a man in her path.

"Come on, you bastards!" Anna roared.

Down on one knee, Jones's eyes returned to normal. He shook the cobwebs of the trance from his head and stood to survey the surrounding carnage. A rider came bearing down on him, but Jones simply dragged him from his horse as warrior spirits swooped in and carried him away, screaming. Catching his breath, Jones scanned the street until he laid eyes on Hanks, running for his life.

Jones mounted a horse and bolted after him. He lunged from the saddle and pinned Hanks to the ground.

"You did this," Jones raged. "You brought death to this place!"

"Leave me be, damn you!" Hanks whined.

"All my life I fought the darkness, kept it held back. So that no man need fear," Jones snatched him up by the collar. "But not you,

Hanks. For you, I step aside from the darkness. I give way to the unending blackness."

Jones ripped the leather cord of bones from his neck. "I give them—you!"

Hanks recoiled as misty, dark forms began to swirl and surround Jones. Their ominous whispers called him by name. Then glowing red eyes and blood-covered claws reached over Jones.

"My God, please, no!" Hanks whimpered.

"Behold the dark gods you prayed to, Hanks," Jones whispered. "Embrace them."

Nameless forms leapt over Jones and dove into Hanks. Even the previously cast out Mangled Creature returned, glowering at Jones before it feasted on Hanks. In seconds, his body withered and shriveled until there was nothing left but a screaming husk, and then... dust.

Jones reverently placed the bones around his neck again and returned to the melee. He found Rodgers pleading on his knees with a Choctaw Spirit before him.

"Please, in the name of God!"

"Wait!" Jones called out.

The Choctaw Spirit paused and turned to Jones. Again, Jones spoke in their language.

"Must they all die?"

"The land must be as it was," the Spirit replied.

"I have returned you to your land," Jones said.

"And now it must be cleansed."

A ball of fire appeared in the Spirit's hand. Jones' mind raced as he looked at Poole.

"Then let me cleanse it," Jones requested. "I will take them from your land."

The Spirit looked down at Rodgers, holding the ball of fire over him. "The fire will cleanse it."

"What if I pledge on my life that no white eyes will lay claim to your land?" Jones asked.

"This you cannot promise," the Spirit said. "The Buffalo speaks. They come like the great storm. My people will be scattered, but many will still call these lands home until the time of the new age."

"Then I will take your people to a new land. The land of the Old Tribes. For those who will follow, I pledge this."

The ball of fire faded as the Spirit moved to Jones.

"Our cousin would swear this?" the Spirit asked.

Jones looked at Odessa, who nodded with eyes of joyous pride. In this, she knew their bond meant so much more to him than words could ever convey. This sealed their union.

"Today I am brother to the Choctaw," Jones proclaimed. "Those who wish to stay may stay in these sacred lands. Those who wish to go, I will lead to the Old Lands. I swear my life to this people."

The Spirit extended his hand, and the ball of fire alighted once more. Jones accepted his hand calmly, unscathed by the flames.

"The bones and the spirit of our people are as one," declared the Spirit, as he laid his hand on Jones' chest. This time, it burned.

"The joys and sorrows of my people are ever with you, and yours are ever with mine."

Jones fell to his knees and cried out. A brand-new necklace appeared around Jones's neck. A sturdy, woven leather cord with Black bones and Choctaw bones united, an unbreakable bond beyond flesh and blood, Native and Moor, as was foretold. The Spirit smiled at Jones and then at Odessa, who could only weep before her ancestor's spirit.

"We walk as brothers, evermore," the Spirit announced.

"In flesh and spirit, evermore," Jones replied.

And as the sunrise cast pink and gold across the horizon, the Spirit smiled and waved at them all before it rode off, evaporating into the ethers. The wailing war cry carried all the spirits back to their rest as they faded with the dawning of the day.

Willa stumbled into the street, her eyes covered in dust, blood, and tears as she screamed.

"Wait, don't leave me!" she cried. "I waited for you! I swore I'd never leave you."

Jones and Odessa turned to her, as she fell to her knees in the dirt, overwhelmed with despair.

"Please, please don't leave me again!" Willa sobbed.

She pounded her tiny fists into the earth before she laid her cheek against the ground. Her spirit had finally broken.

"Please, don't leave me here," she whispered through tears.

Just then, a gentle wind blew across her face. It wrapped around her almost playfully. A scent only Willa could catch filled the air. She gasped as she looked up to see the Choctaw girl that Poole had seen before. But this was no random specter or ghost. This was Willa's childhood friend, the one she missed so dearly. Whose loss Willa had carried with her for decades. She smiled at Willa, and they burst into laughter.

"You didn't leave me!" Willa exclaimed through tears.

The girl ran into Willa's arms and wrapped her up in a sweet embrace. A white light embraced them both, nearly blinding everyone. As it faded, only two young girls remained. The spirits of two lifelong friends who had finally been reunited. They danced until they both vanished in the peach light of the coming sun.

"God bless you, Widow Stanton," Jones whispered.

A giggle only he could hear echoed in the waning breeze. Assessing the danger had passed, Rodgers got to his feet, brushed himself off, and crossed over some dead bodies to Jones.

"Thank God!" Rodgers exclaimed. "You've done it! It's over!"

Jones eyed him smugly, already sensing where this was going.

"I kept my word. As must you," he replied.

"Jones," Rodgers' voice rippled. "You don't just expect me to give up my livelihood? We were all under a great deal of duress."

"So, even though slavery itself is no more," Jones began, " and even though I risked my life on your behalf, you're gon' stand there and renege on our agreement?"

Rodgers swallowed hard. Shifting his feet in the dirt, his mind raced to find a response. "Well, surely we can certainly come to some kind of mutual arrangement."

Jones shook his head and began walking away. He clenched his fist to keep from reaching for his gun. This was something he'd learned to expect from men like Rodgers, men whose greed exceeded their character. Men who preyed on the ignorance of those less fortunate. But what was also true was that there was little Jones could do to make him keep his word, nothing that prevented Rodgers from bending the town to his will the moment Jones left town.

"Man's life is only as good as his word," Jones said. "Lest his life ain't nothing."

"What if I gave you ten slaves to call your own?" Rodgers attempted to bargain. "Two dozen, that would be fair, yes?"

Jones stopped and turned to Rodgers slowly, moving his hand for his gun.

"You should've chosen a profession that helped you lead a long life."

"I beg your par—" Rodgers suddenly struggled to speak.

He looked down and saw his own blood filling his chest as it spilled onto his shirt. And then a gentle hand fell on his shoulder. He jerked awkwardly. His knees buckled as a knife sank deep into his back. Another thrust caused the tip of the blade to break through his chest.

"I choose whose bed I warm," Odessa leaned in close and whispered, twisting the knife.

As Rodgers fell to the ground, Odessa was unaware that a vengeful Gentry was taking aim at her from the side of a building.

"Got you, bitch," Gentry growled.

A loud shot rang out. But it was Gentry whose eyes rolled back in his head. He fell face-first into the dirt with a loud thump. From behind him, Poole emerged from the gun smoke with a wry smile and a smoldering rifle.

"You run your mouth too much, Gentry." Poole hissed and spat on Gentry's back.

Jones waved at Poole, who nodded in his direction. Blood pooled around Rodgers, now dead at Odessa's feet. Fate had finally caught up with his two-timing ways and gutted him like he'd done so many others. He'd gambled one too many times and paid the price for good.

Odessa pushed her hair back and wiped her blade clean as she gave Jones a soft smile.

"I do like the women in this town," Jones smiled back.

SEVENTEEN

It had been a week since that fateful night. A cold, early morning rain had muddied the streets and left puddles that reflected a dismal gray sky. Appropriate for what was to come. This morning would mark the end of one era and the beginning of another. This was to be the last day of Menifee, at least for her residents, who knew it as such.

The plains wind blew through charred frames, the remains of the buildings that weren't burned to the ground days ago. Those left behind had cleaned away most of the carnage, but some things were best left where they were. Most agreed it was a fitting warning to anyone who might have a notion to settle there and should think better of it.

By the time everything and everyone had packed up, there were two caravans of covered wagons. They lined both sides of the street as every man, woman, and able child had busily loaded their belongings, their memories, and their fears to set out and find a new home.

Doc Willis loaded little Virginia onto a wagon next to her mother, Anna. He gave Anna a soft smile, and she smiled back. Some good things grew out of that night. Doc Willis had been a widower for a long time and Anna was a fine woman who always yearned to have a good man at her side. Now there was a chance they both could have a good life.

Poole, still the Sheriff, hobbled his way to one of the lead wagons and ensured that they were packed tight and firmly secured. He looked back over the remains of Menifee, and eventually over at the fresh burial mounds of those who would never leave. He strode over to them. His eyes landed on one grave marker in particular, with a hand-drawn star and a young man's name on top.

"I'm sorry I let you down, Quail," Poole put his hat in hand. "Powerful sorry."

Doc Willis strolled up to join Poole at Quail's grave. He laid a hand on his shoulder.

"Damn shame," Willis shook his head.

The men stood for a moment, knowing they'd never be able to pay their respects again to their friend.

"Looks like we're all set, Sheriff," Willis broke their silence.

"You know you don't have to call me that anymore, Doc."

"People still need to follow someone," Willis reminded him. "And you're still the man wearing the tin star."

Poole pulled off his badge and looked down on it, feeling the weight of what it meant to be called Sheriff like he never had before. And it would be that way for the rest of his life.

"Ain't nothing left here for us, then," Poole sighed. "Let's get them moving."

Poole marched back down Main Street for a final time, waving to the people who still entrusted their lives to him, giving them that assured nod they'd all come to lean on. He reached his own rig and hoisted himself atop the wagon, taking up the reins.

"Move 'em out!" he shouted.

Slowly, the wagons inched their way out of town along the muddy road. It took an hour before the last wagon pulled away from the welcome sign and with nothing more than the creaking of wagon wheels, Menifee was no more. Behind them forever were the ghosts of days gone by, and hopefully the pain that came with them.

On a ridge overlooking their former town, Poole watched from his wagon as the second caravan turned away from them and headed west into the badlands. He felt his heart skip a beat as two riders on black horses broke off and charged up the hill toward him. Poole adjusted his hat and smiled as Jones and Odessa pulled up alongside him. Odessa wore a buffalo skin around her shoulders, good for when it got cold. Jones was dressed in black from head to toe, even a new hat and boots, courtesy of the tailor, thankful to have survived the end of Menifee. It thoroughly amused Poole to contemplate whether Jones would ever get used to the fancier new look. Even so, Jones still wore the necklace of bones, a clear reminder to everyone of exactly who he was.

"Jones. Ma'am," Poole acknowledged them with the tip of his hat.

"Sheriff Poole," Jones chuckled. His friend was stuck with the title.

"I'd like to thank you and your people for lending us a hand," Poole said to Odessa.

"You were never our enemy, Sheriff," she replied.

"Can't say I've been an ally as often as I should, either."

"May the winds be at your back, Sheriff Poole," she smiled.

Odessa trotted off to say her goodbyes. Poole turned his attention to Jones.

"Guess Mexico is no longer in the cards for you."

"You know me, Sheriff," he replied. "I keep my word."

An awkward moment of silence as they looked at one another.

"You never did explain what that darkness was you talked about," Poole asked.

Jones glanced over Poole's shoulder and then back at the wagons. Even now he could still see it, the dark specters that clung in dark corners. Most appeared normal. Some sat right beside the townsfolk, as they patiently waited for that moment when either flesh or spirit would become weak again. For such is the burden of men. And the darkness glared back at Jones. He leaned into his horse with a slight sigh.

"You'll know, in time," Jones said. "But I reckon you know better now."

Poole nodded and said, "His blood cries unto me."

"Is that right?" Jones gave him a surprised look. "Thought you weren't the church type?"

"Just cause I don't attend, don't mean I ain't read it," Poole replied. "My Pa was a minister for a spell."

Jones laughed out loud. "Well, don't that beat all."

"Ain't no cause for you to go making fun of me!" Poole gave him a wounded look.

"On the contrary, Sheriff," Jones laughed. "My daddy was a kind of minister, too, in a way."

Poole beamed at this. Finally, something they shared. Then he laughed too.

"A lot of people owe you their lives," Poole acknowledged. "Shame that can't be repaid."

"Considering how you saved me once, I'd say we're square," Jones replied.

"What about your calling?" Poole asked.

Jones stared out at the caravan moving away below them. His own life had changed forever, too.

"People always seem to find me when I'm needed," Jones said. "That won't change."

Poole gave Jones a somber stare, filled with both sadness and regret.

"How can any man bear what you have seen and not lose his mind?" he asked.

Jones suddenly sensed a kinship between them, realizing that Poole had been touched by the world of spirits that most men never know.

"I could ask the same of you now," Jones replied.

Poole glanced back at the wagons, much the same way Jones had done a few moments ago. For a moment Jones wondered, could he see them too?

"I reckon you could, Jones."

Jones glanced back at Odessa. Poole noted his smile.

"Damn fine woman, that Odessa." Poole said.

"I hope she knows what she's getting into," Jones grinned.

"That's funny. I was about to say the same about you."

Both men shared a hearty laugh. Jones pulled off his glove and stretched his hand to Poole. It was more than a salutation after what they'd been through. This was an act of genuine friendship. Poole may have indeed been the first white man Jones called friend.

"My friends call me Jacob," Jones said.

Poole heartily shook his hand, then dabbed at his eyes.

"Mighty proud to call you friend. But you'll forgive me if I say I hope our paths never cross again."

"Ain't on me to forgive you. This time, I'll make an exception," Jones smiled. "Until we meet again, Sheriff."

"Until then, Jacob."

Jones turned his horse and rode back to Odessa. They waved at Poole's caravan as they headed back down to rejoin their own. Poole watched with an aching heart as the first Black man he called friend rode away into the Badlands. Jones patted his horse softly and glanced over his shoulder to see Poole's wagon slip from view. Something inside him ached and Odessa saw it written on his face. She guided her horse closer to him.

"Troubled, Jones?" she asked as she kicked his leg.

"Thinking about what it would be like to just have a home and a family and not be burdened by this calling to do what I do."

Odessa laughed aloud, which only annoyed Jones.

"I say something funny?" he asked.

"What makes you think you can give me children?" she grabbed her reins tight. "Just look at your horse."

"What the hell is wrong with my horse?" Jones stammered, slightly offended.

"What makes you think you—or it—could catch me?" she smiled before she kicked her horse and charged off.

Jones sat stunned for a moment. Her hair whipped in the wind and her horse's hooves kicked up a cloud of dust at top speed, before he suddenly came to his senses.

"Oh, hell no!" he kicked his horse's ribs. "Come on, girl!"

Odessa yelped aloud as Jones howled behind her.

EPILOGUE

Months passed, and all that remained of the town, once known as Menifee, were abandoned pieces of buildings. Structures that resembled nothing more than standing sticks that weakened every day against the unforgiving wind. What was once a town thriving with life now bore the specter of death on every street in every way.

At the twilight of the day, a black carriage meandered its way past a dangling, faded 'welcome' sign, and into town. Sharp spikes adorned the wheels of the carriage, which were covered in a substance resembling soot. Two dark horses, mouths filled with red foam, heaved hard as they trotted forward. Their exposed ribs rattled as their decaying flesh fell to the ground. Nevertheless, they did their master's bidding.

A small man with graying hair and ragged childlike features pulled against the reins to bring the horses to a stop. He spat blood onto the ground and cast his gaze behind him to the door as it creaked open.

The black heel of a woman's foot hissed as it touched the ground, as if it burned the earth beneath it. She emerged from the carriage—the Inky Figure Jones had faced twice in his lifetime.

But in the fading light of day, her softer features were evident. Her sunken eyes seemed hollow against her dark skin, which shone with an ashen hue behind her lips, painted moist and black.

The Inky Figure strode through what was left of Menifee, past dozens of graves marked with the same date, until she came upon the dusty, charred remains of Collins. She knelt down and pulled a dark glove from her hand, which was nothing more than withered skin pulled tightly around her bones. Dipping a sinewy finger into what remained of Collins, she brought the ash to her mouth. A sinister smile flashed across her face. She gave a slight gasp of pleasure as she suckled the matter with great earnest.

"Ah, dear cousin," she said. "We shall meet again soon."

ACKNOWLEDGEMENTS

A lifetime of people have played a part in me becoming the writer I am, deserve a great deal of thanks for their wisdom and support, and I am forever grateful.

First, I want to thank my elementary school teacher, Janet Witbeck, who saw my imagination as a worthwhile pursuit.

To my aunt, Emma, your library of books was my gateway into this life.

To Professor John Stewart at *The Ohio State University* who gave me the courage to share my voice with the world.

To Jonathan and Tony, my creative brothers in my formative years who were there from the start.

To Steve and Kimberly for all of our crazy days huddled away and writing in Denny Hall.

To my sons, Brandon, Julian, and Evan for all the horror movies you never told your mom I took you to see.

To my wife, Venita, who put up with me while I labored to create this story and still puts up with me.

To music artists Jelly Roll, Rashad, Willie Jones, Rhianna, Fleurie, and Blake Shelton who gave me the soundtrack to write BBJ.

And finally, to the legendary Sidney Poitier for *Buck and the Preacher* and the powerful impression it made on my life.

I owe you all pancakes.

JM

ABOUT THE AUTHOR

Cleveland, Ohio native James Moorer is a Los Angeles-based best-selling author, screenwriter, literary manager, publisher, actor, producer, and director. He is an unflinching storyteller who isn't afraid of the foreboding passenger in the souls of man. He specializes in dark, character-driven horrors and thrillers where the road to hell is paved with good intentions, where the good fight is more than an ideal, and where blood-covered heroes love pancakes.

James is known for his work on "DEATHDATE,""STASIS," and the award-winning films, "THE REAL MAN,""ONLY IN PARIS," and "IN THE DEATHROOM," based on a Stephen King short story. He has optioned several projects and enjoys weekends cruising the coast with his wife, Venita, while searching for the best brunches in Southern California.

For more information: www.jamesmoorer.com

Manager: Jon S. Katzman, KDX Entertainment

www.ingramcontent.com/pod-product-compliance
Lightning Source LLC
Chambersburg PA
CBHW011143310726

48972CB00009B/2835